PETER CORRIS was born in Stawell, Victoria, in 1942. He has worked as a lecturer and researcher in history as well as a freelance writer and journalist, specialising in sports writing. He has written thrillers, a social history of prizefighting in Australia, quiz books, radio and television scripts, and the historical novels *The Gulliver Fortune*, *Naismith's Dominion*, *The Brothers Craft*, and *Wimmera Gold*. He is also the co-author of *Fred Hollows, An Autobiography*.

In 1999 Peter Corris was awarded the Ned Kelly Lifetime Achievement Award by the Crime Writers Association of Australia. His previous Cliff Hardy novel, *The Black Prince*, was shortlisted for Best Australian Crime Novel.

The Other Side of Sorrow is the twenty-third in his successful series of books about Sydney-based private eye Cliff Hardy.

CW00606373

'Cliff Hardy' series

THE OTHER SIDE OF SORROW

A CLIFF HARDY NOVEL

Peter Corris

BANTAM BOOKS
SYDNEY • AUCKLAND • TORONTO • NEW YORK • LONDON

THE OTHER SIDE OF SORROW
A BANTAM BOOK

First published in Australia and New Zealand
in 1999 by Bantam

Copyright © Peter Corris, 1999

National Library of Australia
Cataloguing-in-Publication Entry

Corris, Peter, 1942– .
The other side of sorrow.
ISBN 1 86325 185 5.
I. Title.
A823.3

Transworld Publishers,
a division of Random House Australia Pty Ltd
20 Alfred Street, Milsons Point, NSW 2061

Random House New Zealand Limited
18 Poland Road, Glenfield, Auckland

Transworld Publishers (UK) Limited
61–63 Uxbridge Road, Ealing, London W5 5SA

Random House Inc
1540 Broadway, New York, New York 10036

Cover design by Noel Pennington Design
Main cover photography by Tim Webster Photography, Melbourne
Text designed and typeset in Garamond 11 on 13 by Midland
Typesetters, Maryborough, Victoria
Printed and bound by Griffin Press, Netley, South Australia

10 9 8 7 6 5 4 3

NOTE: The title comes from Helen Garner's
endorsement of Nancy Sawer's story collection,
Travelling Alone (1998)

Acknowledgements

For help in the preparation of this book, thanks to Stan West who gave me some Homebush lore, the taxi driver who took me on a tour of the Olympic sites, Jean Bedford and the tenacious but compassionate editors, Louise Thurtell and Katie Stackhouse.

For Jock Allan, gym partner and raconteur

1

'Hello, Cliff. It's Cyn, as you always used to call me. Cynthia Samuels. I know this must be a bolt from the blue, but I have to see you. I need to tell you something. I'll be in the city tomorrow and I want you to meet me at the cafe in the State Library, say at eleven-thirty. Please, please try to make it. Here's my number in case you can't, but please try.'

I scarcely heard the numbers she recited on the answering machine tape in that strange way people reel off their telephone numbers. Her voice and tone were unmistakable even though I hadn't heard them for more than twenty years. Cyn was my ex-wife and our parting had been as tempestuous as the relationship itself. We got a no-fault divorce under the new law and went our ways. I kept vaguely in touch with Cyn's life through her father who I played a bit of tennis with. But he'd died some years back and that broke the connection.

I played the message again. 'I want you to meet me . . .' That was typical of Cyn. She always expected to get her own way. With me she had, but only for a shortish time. As it turned out, our ideas of how to live were completely different. This had been obscured from us at first. By sex, mainly. Cyn was an architect who either sat in an office or went out to places she was helping to put into strict order. She liked life to follow suit. I was a private detective who spent as little time in my office as possible and most of it out dealing with messes that rarely got completely cleaned up.

When we split up we had virtually no assets. Our equity in the Glebe terrace consisted of the small deposit we'd jointly put down. I took out a personal loan and paid back her half and that was about it. She'd disliked the house and Glebe anyway, and went back to the other side of the harbour. I signed the divorce kit papers she sent me and we spent about five minutes in court establishing that our marriage had irretrievably broken down. We didn't shake hands and wish each other luck. I'd always felt bad about that.

All this and much more came back as I listened to the tape for a third time. Inevitably, I remembered the fights more clearly than the good times. There were plenty of both — screaming matches that almost, but never quite, got physical, at least on my side. Cyn accused me of every crime in the book — neglect, dishonesty, infidelity, drunkenness, irresponsibility. Increasingly, as things got worse between us, the accusations were valid. In the end my failure to show up for 'a talk' which I'd sworn to do was the last straw for Cyn and she left, cleaning the house out of all her possessions.

I remember getting home full of remorse for not

keeping my promise and finding her gone. I immediately went looking for the gin bottle to help me through it, but she'd taken the gin.

The good times were less sharply focused in my memory — beach holidays, dinners, late night walks through Glebe and sexual bouts that left us both exhausted.

On the third run-through I paid more attention to the present than the past. The voice, although recognisable, had changed a bit. Still firm, but not *as* firm, still clear but not *as* clear. And for Cyn to say please three times in a short message was unusual. This made me curious. But I was surprised to find that traces of the old hostility persisted. *Bugger it, why should I put myself out for her?* was one impulse. Against that, she said she had something to tell me and information was my business. I had the phone number written down and I could have called and suggested a meeting in another place at another time. But how petty was that?

As it happened, I didn't have a lot on at the time and after successfully concluding a long-running fraud investigation I was solvent if not flush. That evening I wandered around the house, noting the signs of neglect and decay that advanced and retreated over the years as I spent or withheld money. The house was worth a fair bit now, but I could never bring myself to move. Inertia? Nostalgia? I wasn't sure. As I moved around I kept thinking about Cyn and the short time we'd spent here. Were there any traces left of that time? I laughed when I realised that there was at least one — a missing staircase baluster which I'd grabbed on the way down after Cyn had pushed me. Hard. After a while I gave up and went to bed. The last I'd heard Cyn was living with her advertising executive husband in a Wahroonga mansion and I bet there wasn't a broken baluster in the place.

In the morning I took a good look at myself in the bathroom. I still had all my hair and it was more dark than grey. The cheeks were seamed and the multiple broken nose wasn't beautiful, but the money I'd spent on my teeth had been worthwhile. Plenty of crows' feet, but no jowls yet. A bit soft in the middle but not too bad. I knew it was ridiculous, but I shampooed my hair, shaved closely and put on a clean shirt, newly dry-cleaned pants and brushed lint from my well-worn blazer. No tie.

In these pre-Olympic days, when they're ripping up the city and turning it into a series of holes in the ground and cranes in the air, it makes no sense to take a car into the CBD. The traffic crawls and is diverted into places where you don't want to go. Parking costs a packet and you never know when you're going to be a victim of road rage, or a perpetrator. It was Monday, supposedly a light traffic day, but I wasn't tempted. Some day a politician is going to have to find the guts to ban private cars in the city or institute an odds and evens system. I wasn't holding my breath. There's talk of reinstating a ferry from Glebe to Circular

Quay and I'm looking forward to it. I caught a bus.

As I sat on the bus I looked at my dollar-twenty ticket. Geoff Towers, my accountant, would insist on me submitting it as an expense even if I wasn't on the way to see a client or pursuing an investigation.

'You're riding on public transport, right?' Geoff Towers once said over a similar tiny amount for a rail journey. 'You're seeing things, right? Noting changes in schedules and timetables. Security arrangements or the lack of them more likely. That's a professional activity. You think those consultant arseholes the Tax Office hires don't write off paper clips?'

'How about when I'm having a beer in the Toxteth on a Friday night? Observing humanity.'

'Arguable,' Geoff said. 'Eminently arguable.'

That train of thought led me back to Cyn and what she had to tell me. After telling me goodbye she'd had nothing else to tell me for twenty-plus years. 'I hope I never see you again,' was one of the things she'd said towards the end. Well she hadn't, apart from our moment in court. In the time between the split and the divorce I'd tried often to contact her but she'd thrown up a high wall. She'd told our few mutual friends not to talk to me about her and instructed them to tell me not to ask. In all the time I was with her I never knew Cyn to change her mind. This had to be something serious.

Libraries have changed in the last twenty-five years more than most institutions. They used to be gloomy, wood-panelled places with a musty smell and tight-lipped women in twinsets. Now they're brightly lit, computerised, and the senior reference librarian is likely to be sporting tattoos and a lip ring. The cafe was below decks in the library but natural light flooded down from a massive lightwell. That was welcome. Since I incurred some damage to the cornea of my left eye I'm slow to adapt to changes in the light. Too dim and I'm fumbling, too bright and I'm dazzled. As it was, in this bright space with very few of the tables occupied, I spotted Cyn almost straight away and before she spotted me. Always an advantage, that. The tables were grouped around an indoor garden and waterfall. Cyn was sitting near the centre of the place. She was reading with the book held well out in front of her. That was a sign that she was short-sighted. Cyn would be too vain to wear glasses in public. I pulled up and looked at her. The hair was still blonde and lux-uriant; her wide mouth was closed firmly and the sculptured features that had thrilled me were still in evidence. Always slim, she looked even thinner in her late forties than she'd been in her twenties. That was Cyn. When she was slender she'd tried to be skinny. Well, she'd made it.

'Hello, Cyn.'

I'd snuck up on her, gumshoeing it. But you couldn't faze Cyn. She slowly lowered the book and levelled her blue eyes at me.

'Cliff,' she said, 'Sit down.'

It was always like that. Just when I thought I'd got the drop on her in some way she'd fake me out. She was paler than I remembered and there was something frail-looking about her neck bones showing above the collar of the white silk blouse. She was wearing a blue linen jacket, almost certainly the top half of a suit. The shoes and bag would match in the same way the string of pearls and earrings matched. The pearls were a mistake though, they drew attention to that fragile neck.

I sat and undid my blazer. 'You're thinner,' I said.

'I'm older.'

'Most people get fatter. I have.'

'You're all right. Better than I expected. That nose's seen some wear and tear though.'

I grunted. 'What about a drink?'

'Same old Cliff. What time d'you start these days?'

'I gave up spritzers with breakfast a while ago.' I held out my hands to show my nicotine stain-free fingers. 'And the fags.'

She laughed and as the skin tightened over her face I thought, *Christ, she really is thin. Too bloody thin.*

'Me, too,' she said. 'Yes, let's have a drink. They serve wine by the glass here. By the *big* glass.'

A teenage waitress in a white blouse, long skirt and the heavy shoes they like to wear, arrived and we ordered glasses of white wine and open sandwiches. We'd both been heavy smokers when we were together and now we exchanged stories about how we'd managed to quit. When the food and drink came I attacked mine as a way of not asking her why we were here. I wanted her to explain herself. Still fencing, as in the old days. She made a brave show of drinking her wine and eating but I could tell it was a battle. But she was the old Cyn still, not going on the back foot. She asked me about my business and if I'd kept the house. I said business was okay and I had.

'It must be worth a bit,' she said, playing with an olive and a cube of cheese.

Eat it, I thought. *Put some meat on your bones*.

'I like it too much to sell it,' I said. 'I like the memories — good and bad.'

She nodded and pushed the olive and the bit of cheese around. I felt that I was losing the fencing match so I said, 'I was sorry to hear about your dad. I had a lot of time for him.'

'I know. I don't suppose you heard about my husband?'

That stopped me. I took a drink and realised my glass was almost empty while hers had barely been touched. What the hell, I thought. I reached over and tipped half of it into my mine. 'No,' I said. 'What?'

She lifted an eyebrow when I pinched her wine and again the movement emphasised her lack of flesh. 'Colin died about six months after my father. Heart attack. He worked too hard, didn't sleep, didn't exercise . . .'

'I'm sorry. Really. You were together for a long time. Kids and all. That's tough.'

She put her fork down, lifted what was left of her wine and wet her lips before putting the glass down and pushing it over to me. 'I'm dying, Cliff,' she said.

8

Her eyes were fixed on mine as she spoke and her voice was firm. I knew she was speaking the truth.

'Cyn. No.'

'Yes. Breast cancer. I've had 'em both off. Radiation, chemotherapy.' She reached up and touched her hair. 'This is a wig. Fooled you, eh?'

I suddenly choked-up. 'Cyn . . .'

She reached over and touched my hand. Her touch was as cold as if she was already dead. I'd seen it before — the dying comforting the living — and I'll never understand it. I shook my head. 'Fuck it,' I said. 'This isn't right. Not you.'

She smiled. 'Yeah, fuck it. But it's true. I've only got a few months, if that. Probably less. I was in seeing the Macquarie Street man today. No hope.'

'There's clinics. Mexico. Germany . . .'

'I've been to all the clinics I can take. I've got a good doctor. He'll see me off when it gets too bad.' She laughed. 'That's all right. It's too bloody soon but it'll be easy, whereas the rest of you never know how it'll come, do you?'

I gulped some wine. 'That's right. Jesus, Cyn, I . . .'

'Bear up, Cliff. We've got a bit to get through here. It could be worse. Both the kids . . . my kids, are old enough to cope. My mother's still around to help. You remember her. She's a toughie.'

'Sure.'

'I used to pick up the ódd scrap about you from Dad, but not since he died. I was curious about you but I couldn't show it too much. Colin was jealous of you.'

'Of me?'

'Yes. He was one of those indoorsmen who secretly yearned to be an outdoorsman. When we fought, as we often did, he'd say things like, "I suppose your private eye never made a mistake."'

'Hah.'

'Right. You made plenty. But I kept a couple of books you gave me and that bullet thing. You remember.'

I remembered. I'd brought back the brass casing of an artillery shell from Malaya. Polished up, it made a nice vase.

Cyn made another attempt to eat but gave up. 'Colin hated that. I'm a bit of a bitch as you know. I used it against him. Don't get me wrong, the marriage was fine, but married people play games. You know.'

I knocked back some more white. If this went on I was going to need a bottle. 'Colin needn't have worried. After the time in court I never laid eyes on you again. Anyway, indoorsmen make more money than outdoorsmen.'

'That's the sort of half-smart thing you used to say. It made me mad.'

'I know.'

She leaned forward across the table and I could feel the intensity in her. 'Tell me, Cliff, are you . . . in a relationship at present? I assume there've been a few over the years, but . . .'

I desperately needed something to do with my hands and if there had been cigarettes available I would have taken one. I put both hands on the

wine glass and swilled what was left of its contents. 'Look, Cyn,' I said. 'You've told me about
the cancer and it's just about the worst thing I can
remember hearing. But where's this going?'

She leaned back and drew a deep breath. The
effort of doing it seemed to cause her pain and
she aged ten years as she fought for composure.
'Cliff,' she said softly. 'I was pregnant when we
split up. I dithered until it was too late to have an
abortion. The child was born. A girl. You're her
father.'

2

My first reaction was disbelief. This had to be some kind of fantasy, a product of the treatment she was having or a mental aberration associated with the disease or the prospect of death. It couldn't be true. Cyn read me right immediately.

'You don't believe me.'

'I'm sorry, no.'

'It's true, Cliff. You remember how it was. I hated you. I wanted nothing more to do with you, ever. It'd all gone so terribly wrong. Everything we'd planned had turned to shit.'

I nodded.

'I had the baby in Bathurst at a Catholic hospital. I used my own name and I didn't tell anyone about it. Not even my parents. Look.'

She opened her handbag, took out a sheet of paper and thrust it at me. It was an admission record from St Margaret's Hospital for Women dated about seven months after our final breakup. Cynthia Louise Weimann had been admitted 'close to confinement' and discharged eight days later.

I was still resistant, almost hostile. 'It proves you

12

were pregnant, I guess. It doesn't prove there was a child.'

'I know this isn't easy for you, but it's true.'

She handed over another document. This was a notification, dated three months back, that Mrs Cynthia Samuels had put her name on the register of women who had given a child up for adoption. The sex of the child was given as female, the place of birth was Bathurst and the adoption date was four days after the date of the hospital admission. I'd done some work in this area once or twice. The purpose of the register was to allow adopted children to locate their natural parents if they wished. They had the option. I folded the paper and handed it back. My hand was shaking, but I still didn't want to believe it.

'Cyn. You must have been through hell . . .'

'I've seen her, Cliff,' she said. 'I've *seen* her!'

She wept quietly and I comforted her as best I could. I got another glass of wine and Cyn had mineral water. With an effort she composed herself and told me that she'd caught sight of a particular young woman several times in recent weeks. She was convinced that this woman was watching her. I was still sceptical.

'You haven't spoken to her?'

'No. I've never been able to get close enough. She sort of . . . slips away.'

'What makes you think she's . . . who you think she is? It could be someone, I don't know, sympathetic but not sure whether to approach you. Or . . .'

She shook her head. 'Cliff, she's the living

image of your sister Eve twenty-four years ago. I'm telling you she could be her twin. I *know* she's our daughter.' She scrabbled in her bag and came up with a photograph. It showed Eve in jeans, boots and a sweater smiling into the camera. Short dark hair, thin, beaky nose, wide mouth, my sister was arresting rather than pretty. She was close to 180 centimetres tall and when she was young athletics and surf swimming kept her lean. She's heavier now which doesn't hurt her golf. She plays off eight at Moore Park.

'It's a copy,' Cyn said. 'I had you and me cropped out of it. Don't know why I still had it. D'you remember where it was taken? A picnic we all went on in Centennial Park.'

'No. You say this woman resembles Eve?'

'I've only caught glimpses of her. But I'd say she's identical. Oh, shit!' Her hand flew up to her face and I saw how thin her wrist was, with the blue veins showing through. 'Eve doesn't have a daughter, does she?'

'No. Two sons.'

'God. I realise I haven't thought this through enough. Do *you* have any children, Cliff? I mean, other children . . .'

I drank some wine. 'You didn't think of that possibility either, did you? Why not?'

You couldn't keep Cyn on the defensive for long. She drank some of her mineral water and got a fair bit of energy into a snort. 'You were always a selfish bastard, Cliff. There was only barely enough space in your life for a lover. What with the crims and cops and other low-lifes. There certainly wasn't enough for a wife. I doubt you'd ever have entertained the idea of having kids. Tell me I'm wrong.'

I had to admit she was right. The only really serious relationships I'd had since Cyn were with Helen Broadway and Glen Withers. Helen had a child and a troubled marriage and in the end she'd opted for the status quo. Glen was a career woman all the way. I'd felt comfortable with arrangements like those.

'You're right,' I said. 'Maybe you heard from your dad about Hilde Stoner. The tenant I had for a while. She married Frank Parker, who's —'

'A policeman. Yes, I heard. So?'

'I'm a sort of pagan godfather to their son, Peter. That's as close as I thought I'd ever get to parenthood.'

'Ah, you're admitting the possibility that you've fathered a child. Christ, you're a hard sell, Cliff.'

'In my business you have to be. Look, Cyn, what d'you think's going on here?'

'That's typical of you. Analysis rather than engagement.'

'That's me.'

'All right. I think she applied for her birth certificate. Adoptees can do that since the act was changed in 1990. Did you read that book by Charmian Clift's illegitimate daughter?'

'No. I read *My Brother Jack* though — her husband's best book. Sorry, Cyn. Go on.'

'I think she applied for her original birth certificate and got my name from it.' She looked directly at me. 'Don't worry. There was no name for the father. I didn't have to give it.'

I think it was at that moment that I started to believe all this might be true.

Cyn went on to say that she asked the appropriate authorities whether her child had applied for her birth certificate or made enquiries about her, but the rules didn't allow for that information to be given out.

'That's right,' I said. 'I've done a little bit in this line. The idea is to protect the adoptee — in case the parent's a drunk or a bludger. If you're right about this, Cyn, why wouldn't she make herself known to you? You're obviously affluent and respectable. You live in a big house and drive a flash car. You've got a tennis court, I'm told, and isn't there a boat or two?'

'Stop it, Cliff. Don't be such a shit. If she — Jesus, I don't even know her name — if she got onto me in the last few months she'd have seen a woman wasting away. I spend most of my time going to doctors. I don't drive any more; I don't have the strength. I sold the house and the boat after Colin died and put most of the money in trust for the kids. I live in a unit in Crows Nest. It's nice but nothing special. The thing is, if she's been keeping an eye on me in that time she's probably seen me faint twice in public and once . . .'

She shook her head, took a deep breath and forced the words out. 'She might have seen me throw up in the gutter.'

The tears came again and I watched helplessly while she dabbed at her eyes. She seemed to have to gather every ounce of her strength to do just

16

that much. I had the feeling that she was just about all through for the day at a bit past noon. It made me forget all the animosities and injuries of the past and want to do anything I could to help her. Or almost anything. Despite the anger and anguish I felt on her behalf, I was still focused on the main game — the possibility that we'd had a child.

Perhaps Cyn was right in thinking selfishness had kept me childless. I preferred to believe it was something else — a recognition that my failure to sustain relationships and my erratic, hazardous, financially chancy lifestyle made me a poor bet as a father. More than once I'd pulled back from involvement with women who seemed primed for motherhood, not wanting to disappoint them. But I'd also worn childlessness as a sort of badge, a flag of independence and self-sufficiency. All that was ingrained by now and I was reluctant to surrender it.

Cyn summoned up strength from somewhere and looked directly at me. Her eye makeup was smudged and she had a blurred, off-centre look that gave everything she said an extra weight. 'I wouldn't blame her for holding back. Who would want a broken down woman with no tits who chucks in the street for a mother?'

'Don't, Cyn.'

'Damn you, Cliff Hardy. Don't you pity me. Don't you dare pity me. I've had a good life. I was a successful architect. There're buildings in this bloody city that'll last longer than you and every-one else alive. They prove I was good. I've got two wonderful children and a grandchild . . .' She

17

stopped and stared straight through me as if she was looking into another dimension where faces and walls and pillars didn't matter. 'I've got a grandchild on the way. It'll be touch and go whether I'll live to see it.'

The waitress came to take our plates. I'd eaten most of my meal but Cyn's was barely touched.

'Was there something wrong ma'am?'

Cyn shook her head.

'Will there be anything else, sir?'

'No, thank you. Nothing else.'

She cleared the table, leaving the dregs of our drinks, and beat a retreat. I knew what she was thinking — *a middle-age marriage break up, bad news*. She wasn't to know that she was right in a way, except that the break-up had happened before she was born.

'I'm not poor,' Cyn said. 'I can pay you.'

'What?'

'I can pay for your services. That blazer's seen better days, so has the shirt. You're obviously not rolling in money.'

That was the old Cyn. On the attack. Somehow, though, it seemed sad and I didn't rise to the bait as I would have in the old days. I finished the wine. It tasted sour.

'What d'you want me to do?'

'I want you to keep a watch on me for a few days. What do you call it? A surveillance. And when she appears I want to meet her. I want to talk to her. I want to find out about her. Help her if she needs it, be happy if she doesn't. I want to meet our child, Cliff. Before I die.'

3

I said I'd do it. Cyn gave me the photo of Eve saying that 'our daughter' so much resembled her that I could use the photo in my enquiries. She described the woman in as much detail as she could. Short, dark hair, casual clothes, quick movements. Cyn had seen her three or four times, always in the vicinity of her unit in Crows Nest — at a bus stop, through a shop window, standing on the other side of the road. She thought she'd seen her in a van parked opposite her building but she couldn't be sure.

'What kind of van?'

'Blue and other colours.'

'C'mon, Cyn.'

'I don't know about vans. It wasn't new. I'm tired, Cliff. I have to go home.'

'I'd drive you except that I didn't bring my car into town.'

'It's all right, I'll get a cab. Anyway, we shouldn't be seen together. You have to be as good as she is at keeping your distance.' She dabbed at some perspiration that was breaking out on her upper lip and looked intently at me.

'What?' I said.

'I was just wondering whether she'd see a resemblance between herself and you. You and Eve're pretty much alike as I recall.'

'Come off it, Cyn. I've been knocked about too much to resemble anyone but myself. Besides, she won't see me until I want her to.'

'I suppose that's right. You must be good at what you do by now. How is Eve, anyway?'

'Fine. She just got made redundant from the CES. Golden handshake — more time for golf.'

Cyn's eyes were glazing over the way many people's do at the mention of golf. But in her case it was exhaustion.

'Good,' she said. 'I liked her. I hope . . .'

'What?'

'I hope our daughter is as nice as your sister. That'd be fine. I know this is hard for you. We didn't part friends, did we? More like enemies. I hated you and I think you hated me. I nursed that hate for a long time but it's well and truly gone now. I'm too tired and sick to hate. It takes everything just to stay alive. This is unfinished business for me and I've sort of . . . forgiven us both for what we did to each other. I need you to find her.'

'I have to be honest with you, Cyn. I'll give it my very best. I'm impressed by what you say you want to do if she shows. But I'm still sceptical. I can't help it.'

Cyn sighed. 'That's all right. You're sceptical about everything except that Tommy Burns beat Jack Johnson in 1901.'

She had it the wrong way around and the year

was 1908, but it was a brave try. 'That's right,' I said.

'I'll walk down to the shops every morning and every afternoon for the rest of this week. At ten o'clock and two o'clock, say. You keep watch. As for what you do when she appears, I'll leave it up to you. For all your macho bullshit, Cliff, you're not stupid. I trust you to do it right. You've got something invested here, even if you don't want to think so.'

Born and raised in Maroubra and spending most of my adult life in Glebe, to me the north side of the harbour has always seemed like foreign territory. The light is different and the people likewise. They seem more suburban and less secure than those on the other side. I'm not sure it was such a good idea to build the bridge.

I cleared the decks in my office and mounted the surveillance in Crows Nest as Cyn had directed. I tracked her by foot on her slow progress from her unit down the street to the shopping centre. When we were together Cyn had boundless energy. She could work without sleep for forty-eight hours and play pretty hard, too. She was a good, all-round sportswoman and I had trouble keeping up with her in a beach sprint or a swimming pool. It broke my heart to see her now. Bundled in a heavy coat that concealed her gauntness, she still walked erect. But it was with an effort and every movement and gesture had slowed right down.

In the afternoons particularly, I wondered if she

21

was going to be able to make it; to keep up the charade of window-shopping, browsing and buying odd items. She did it by an effort of will and her performance was faultless. She gave not the slightest indication that she was aware of my presence. I flatter myself I was hard to spot, but she knew and no-one would be able to tell. On the Wednesday night, with no sign of the young woman, I phoned.

'Nothing,' I said. 'Not a cracker.'

'Be patient. It might take a while.'

'How are you feeling? It looks like an effort for you.'

'I'm all right. I can hold out for a while longer.'

The next day a tall, gangly youth with shoulder-length hair parked a battered Honda Civic outside Cyn's building and went in. I watched with no particular interest — until he emerged with Cyn and helped her into the car. Her son, I assumed. He drove her to the shops and carried her bags to the car. They stopped and had coffee on the way back. He seemed attentive and considerate. They laughed a good deal and Cyn appeared to draw strength from him. He took her home, stayed a while, then sat in his car with his head on the steering wheel for quite a few minutes before he drove off. Although I was interested in the interaction between mother and son and moved by his obvious love for her, I still kept a sharp lookout for the girl. Nothing.

One day to go on the agreed arrangement. I was troubled by the thought that I couldn't continue this deal indefinitely. A couple of messages on the answering machine and a couple of faxes demanded attention and promised money. It was early in July, and the accounts kept over from the old financial year were coming in. More troubling were the conflicting thoughts I was having about the whole matter. I wondered what Cyn's two legitimate children would think about the possible existence of a half-sibling. And what the legal implications might be. Along with that, having seen the bond between Cyn and her son, I felt a pang about having nothing remotely like that in my own life. The corollary of that was obvious, if disturbing — did I have a daughter? Did I want or need one?

Friday morning. I was late getting to the gym and had to rush my workout. I wasn't quite a gyma-holic but getting close, and I was annoyed by having to cut back. Still testy, I slotted into my parking spot, checked my watch and waited for Cyn to come out. The sky was overcast and there was a cold wind and the threat of rain. Maybe Cyn would give it a miss and I could go back and do a few more reps on the pec deck. I should have known better. She came out right on time, wrapped in her heavy coat and carrying an umbrella. She looked frail, as if the wind could blow her over. It made me angry to think what this person was putting her through, if indeed there was a person. I was beginning to work back to my original theory about a fantasy induced by drugs or despair. I crawled along, keeping her in sight, until it was time to park and continue on foot.

23

Cyn went into a newsagency and bought a magazine and a scratchie. She used a nail file on the ticket and I saw the pleased, almost childlike, expression on her face when she saw the result. I stared, fascinated; it was an action so unlike anything I would have expected from Cyn that it took all my attention. As a result, I almost missed the girl. It was just a glimpse as she moved quickly away but it was enough to register two things — her contempt at what she'd seen and the uncanny resemblance to my sister as she once was. She was about the same height and build and moved with the same long, fluid stride. That stride was taking her rapidly away from me into the thick Friday crowd as I skirted people waiting in a bus queue and swore as a van shot out of a lane in front of me.

I ran when the lane was clear and saw her well ahead, moving quickly through the crowd, her dark head bobbing. I was fifty metres behind her and gaining when she opened the passenger door of a Kombi van that looked as if it had been painted by John Lennon on acid. I sprinted. No hope of stopping the van but maybe I could get close enough to read the number. I stopped, squinted and read the letters and digits aloud, repeating them several times before scribbling them on my palm with a ballpoint. I was uncertain about one of the numbers. It could have been a five, but perhaps it was a three. Not a bad result under the circumstances. People in the street looked at me and edged away. I didn't blame them. You can't be too careful about out-of-breath men talking to themselves and writing things on their skin.

I walked back the way I came and found Cyn waiting for me outside the newsagency.

'You ran off. You saw her, didn't you?' she said.

'I saw *someone*.'

'Oh, God.'

She swayed and I had to grab her to stop her falling. I was shocked at how thin her arms were and she weighed next to nothing. She was a fully-grown woman but she felt like a child as I helped her walk slowly back to my car. She said nothing until we reached her building, then she turned to me. Her blue German eyes were a washed out pale grey and there were two hectic spots in her cheeks.

'You lost her, didn't you?'

'Not exactly. She got into a van and I got its number.' I showed her the writing on my hand; it had run a bit from perspiration. 'I can trace it. Maybe.'

'What d'you mean, maybe?'

'Cyn, she wasn't driving. I can trace the owner, but who's to say the owner was even driving. Young people borrow and lend cars all the time.'

'It's something though. I know you'll be able to find her. Thanks, Cliff.'

'Don't thank me yet. Wait a bit.'

'She was looking at me, wasn't she?'

'Right.' I wondered whether to tell her in detail what had happened. How would she take it? I decided that she wanted everything she could get,

25

needed it. 'She saw you buy the ticket and scratch it. I have to tell you she wasn't impressed.'

'Wasn't she? Well, that's too bad. You know I had a feeling that she was close. More than a feeling — I *knew* she was there, and I wanted to stand still and do something to give you a chance to look around properly. I guess it worked.'

'I guess it did. How much did you win?'

'Oh, a hundred dollars. I'll give it to Geoffrey. You saw him the other day.'

'Yes. Seemed like a good kid.'

'He is. Cliff — you saw her. You must have been fairly close at one point . . .'

'She had her back to me most of the time.'

'Cliff.'

I gave in. 'OK — you're right. She bears a remarkable resemblance to Eve. Moved like her as well.'

'Moved?'

'Eve was a champion schoolgirl sprinter. She could lick me over a hundred yards. She had this long stride. Quite different from the way they run now. This girl moved the same way.'

'Thank you. You'll follow this up and keep me informed?'

'Of course. Can you manage? D'you want me to call someone. Your son?'

'No, I'll be all right after a rest.'

'I'll see you up there.'

'No. I couldn't bear you to see how I live. The place is awash with pills and things to throw up into. If you want to help me, just *find* her. Please.'

'How will your kids cope with this, if it turns out to be true?'

'How will you?'

'I don't know.'

'Well I don't know about them either. It's not the sort of situation you can cite precedents for. We'll all in the shit together, as you might say.'

I wondered whether I should tell her about the freak wagon — it had sported a Nimbin Mardi Grass sticker and an old one with Porky Pig in a police uniform — and what that might imply about the sort of company the woman was keeping. I decided against. Cyn eased herself out of the car and managed to give the door a healthy slam. She crossed the road with her backbone ramrod straight and I watched her use her security card on the gate and disappear into her own world — what was left of it.

4

I used the mobile to call my contact in the Roads and Traffic Authority and negotiate a fee — all done in a long-established encrypted fashion. Corruption has its place in the scheme of things. She said she'd get on it immediately. I gave her my mobile number and the numbers at home and the office.

'Important, huh? Xerox.' This was a signal that she knew the call wasn't being monitored. How they can be sure I don't know, but they do.

'Very.'

'I should've gone higher.'

'Remember ICAC.'

'Fuck ICAC. Be back to you soon.'

I drove home thinking that of all the strayed, absent, missing, absconding person quests I'd ever been on, this was the strangest. The day turned foul. The rain bucketed down and the traffic became sluggish apart from the odd cowboy confident of his vision and his radials. I drifted back into Glebe and had lunch at the cafe at the corner of Glebe Point Road and Broadway where a string quartet plays on Friday and Saturday nights. Glebe has changed since Cyn lived here.

I drove home and picked up the slightly damp mail from the slightly leaky letterbox. Although I hadn't seen it for so long I recognised Cyn's handwriting on one of the letters. There was no mistaking that precise backhand. I ripped it open and swore when I saw that as well as a note it contained a cheque for $3000. The cheque fell to the floor as I read the note:

Dear Cliff

Don't be offended. I know this business won't be easy for you, but I want you to treat it as a job as much as you can. I know you're good at your job and that you love it. I hated it as you know, but that's ancient history.

Please do your very best. You never know, we might have done something right after all.

My first impulse was to tear up the cheque but I resisted it. A private enquiry agent needs a client to validate his activities and there's no better validation than money. The rules state that there should be a signed contract as well, but who ever heard of a game where everyone played by the rules? I put the cheque away in my wallet. When I got to the office I'd open a file labelled 'Samuels' and put the cheque and the note and a copy of the photograph of Eve in it.

Waiting for the call from the RTA, I made coffee and sat looking out at the rain and trying to find other explanations for the woman who was watching Cyn, or other identities for her. Both my parents were only children so there were no first cousins resembling Eve or myself to consider. I was as sure as any man who'd led a reasonably active sex life can be that I'd fathered no children. The question was — had Eve ever had an illegitimate child? I thought it highly unlikely. As a teenager Eve entered a god-bothering phase that lasted until she went to university at the age of twenty-two. She was evangelical and puritanical until she plunged into left-wing politics in her first year. She married Luke, a fellow radical, in her second year and they had the first of their two sons within a year of that. I'd found Eve the Christian pretty hard to take, but I'd kept in touch with her. I saw more of her after she swapped the Bible for Gramsci. I didn't take Gramsci on board any more than I had the Bible, but it made her easier to make fun of. I couldn't see where Eve could've squeezed in a kid.

A doppelgänger? Sure, they exist, but why would my sister's doppelgänger be watching my ex-wife? The world is crazy, but not that crazy.

The call came through as I was contemplating making a second pot of coffee as a way of heading off the impulse to have a drink. Like many people in this suspicious age, I tend to use the answering machine to screen calls, but this time I picked up.

'Xerox and bingo, Cliff.'

This meant that the call was unmonitored and that the vehicle wasn't registered to some subsidiary of some other string of companies that would make the enquiry amount to a paper chase.

'Tell me.'

'Damien Talbot, unit 3, number 12, George Avenue, Homebush. Age twenty-six. The vehicle was purchased a year ago for two thousand five hundred dollars from a dealer in Homebush. Must be a bomb.'

I grunted. 'Anything else?'

'Your meter's ticking.'

'Remember ICAC.'

'Fuck ICAC. Yep, our Damien has a shitload of unpaid parking tickets out on him, plus an unroadworthy citation. As we speak, being followed up by the boys and girls in blue.'

'Thank you.'

'Up yours. Good punting.'

This was a reference to the method of payment — a deposit in her TAB account. I hung up and studied my notes. I doubted that Cyn would like what I'd turned up so far, particularly the location. Cyn used to regard Leichhardt as the western suburbs and so beneath contempt.

Homebush was much further west.

I'd never spent much time in Homebush, had hardly ever been out there. Despite the attractive name, as far as I knew — and a quick check of an old *Gregory's* confirmed it — the place was a bit of a wasteland. Homebush Bay was muddy and mangrove-ringed; there was a brickworks, an abattoir and a huge rubbish dump in the middle of some secondary-growth bushland. The Flemington saleyards were nearby and it was said that escaped pigs from the saleyards had gone feral on the dump and in the bush and were a risk to life and limb. For many years the pub on Parramatta Road, adjacent to the saleyards, was known as the Sheep Shit Inn.

George Avenue was a short street running up-hill. From the top there would once have been a view across the bush towards the dam and what lay beyond, now the view was of hundreds of hectares of development for the Olympic Games. Brand new roads with pristine kerb and guttering gleaming in the rain; towering steel and cement structures resembling, at distance, the Pompidou Centre; massive earthmoving equipment reshaping the terrain; kilometres of orange tape and temporary barriers; vast tracts of bare earth and not a blade of grass in sight. Here and there the past had been preserved. The dam still existed and what looked like the brickworks. Some trees remained, but there was nowhere for a feral pig to hide. Despite the heavy rain the work was still going on. Bulldozers and backhoes were moving and cranes were swinging their loads.

I turned my attention to the undistinguished block of cream-brick flats at number 12. A three-storey 1950s job and showing its age, with rust stains around the drainpipes and moss in the mortar. These days we forget that most people didn't have cars in the '50s and blocks of flats like these made little provision for them. It looked as if there was space for three or four cars at most, the rest would have to park in the street. I wasn't surprised that the psychedelic van wasn't in evidence — enquiries are rarely that easy. There

32

were twelve letter boxes and the junk mail sticking out of number 3 wasn't a promising sign.

Security was non-existent — the '50s again — and I walked in the front door, located unit 3 at the back and knocked loudly. Nothing. I pressed my ear to the door but got none of the noises of occupation — voices, radio, TV, vacuum cleaner — just the silence that means empty. The lock was pickable but it was a bit early in the proceedings for that. I knocked at number 4 opposite. No response. Likewise at number 2, but the door of number 1 swung open so quickly that I guessed the occupant had been waiting for me. A looker-outer of windows, an ear to the ground type. That could be good.

She was somewhere between middle-aged and older and trying hard to stay on the right side of the divide. She was medium tall, heavily built but holding it well, with considerable undergarment help, in a short, tight skirt and snug-fitting, ribbed, rollneck sweater. She was expertly made up, her hair was attractively arranged and the way she leaned against the door jamb suggested that standing in doorways wasn't new to her.

'I thought you might be here for me,' she said. 'But even the shy ones don't knock on all the other doors first.'

Her broad smile invited me to smile in turn. 'Not today, I'm afraid, I'd like to talk to you, though.'

'Cop?'

I shook my head and showed her my licence.

'Cop,' she said. She glanced at her watch. 'Well,

I guess my 3.30's not coming. I can spare you some time. We can see how we go. Come in, Clifford.'

I winced at the name, but it was encouraging that she was a quick study. Stepping into her flat from the shabby passage was like moving from economy up to business class. The room was tastefully and unfussily furnished with just enough touches — velvet cushions, Balinese-looking wall hangings, a waft of incense — to suggest that things could get interesting further inside.

She pointed to a chair but I shook my head and stood just inside the room. She chuckled and dropped smoothly onto the couch, drawing her legs together, knees up high. She had good legs in sheer black stockings. Medium heels. 'I'm Annette, Clifford,' she said. 'From the look of you I'd say you've been around, so I'm not going to pretend I'm a chiropodist.'

'More into counselling?'

She smiled. 'I'm on the older woman game. If I'd known how profitable and easy it was I'd have taken it up long ago.'

'Good for you, Annette. Less of the Clifford, if you don't mind. Cliff'll do. I'm interested in the tenant of number 3, Damien Talbot.'

'Mmm. Young. Tall. Good-looking. Long hair. Limps a bit. That him?'

'Sounds right. He drives a Kombi van painted the colours of the rainbow.'

She snapped her fingers. Her nails were long, red. 'That's him. Good. You look like trouble. If I can give him some, I will.'

'How's that?'

'Little shit booked an appointment with me and then couldn't get it up. I gave him the name of one of those male clinics. He went nuts and tried to stand over me. I won't take that. My bloke broke one of his thumbs. By accident. That discouraged him.'

This was worse than I'd expected and I sat down to absorb it.

'Not what you wanted to hear, eh?'

'No. When was this?'

'Let's think. Haven't seen them for a couple of weeks. Say, three weeks ago.'

I took the photo of Eve from my wallet and showed it to her. 'When you say them, d'you mean this woman?'

She scarcely glanced at it. 'Yep, that's her. Poor kid. She looks like she deserves better than him, but you never can tell.'

'Do you know her name?'

'No. I never had much to do with them apart from that one time and that was enough for me. Come to think of it I did hear a name. From him, that is. Melly? Molly? Something like that.

'Well, I can see why you're worried. About her being with him I mean. Bloody good-looking and charming with it, but a real nasty streak. He speaks well. You know, good grammar and all. But it's an act.'

'An act?'

'Yeah. Like he's acting and the real him is something else. Look, I love a chat but I'm running a business here. I can't see how I can help you.

They did a flit, the agent tells me, so you won't get a forwarding address.'

'Just anything you know could be a help.'

She looked at her watch again. 'Like what?'

'Their movements. Did they go to work?'

She laughed. 'Not likely. Dole bludgers for sure. I mean him. I saw her reading at the bus stop a couple of times. Could be a student.'

'So, what did they do with themselves? Did they have any friends in the flats here? Is there someone else who might know something?'

She shook her head. 'Scarcely ever here. Oh, there is one thing. That's if I've still got it. Hang on.'

She went out to the kitchen and came back with a leaflet. 'She put these in the letterboxes. I stuck it up on the fridge. I hate all that Olympics carry on, but I suppose it'll be good for business. Take a look.'

The leaflet was cheaply produced, with a grainy photograph showing a narrow tree-fringed waterway. It was headed SAVE TADPOLE CREEK and went on to solicit support for the Friends of the Creek's on-site picket preventing the diversion and piping of the stream.

'I haven't heard anything about this, have you?'

She shrugged. 'They've probably hushed it up. I've got a client who works on one of the projects over there. He says you wouldn't believe the rackets going on. And nobody wants to stir the possum. Look, I'm sorry, but I don't have time to chat about politics and such. Now, if you'd like to make a booking I'll give you my number.'

I stood and tapped the paper. 'Can I keep this?'

'Sure.'

'I'll write the number on the back.'

She gave it to me and I thanked her.

'No trouble. I hope you call.'

'One thing, Annette, if you don't mind my asking.' I gestured at the room in general. 'You've got this looking very nice, but why here?'

She steered me towards the door. 'A lot you know. The richer they are the more down-market they like the neighbourhood to be. And somewhere wifey-poo would never ever go.'

5

I sat in the car and thought over what I'd learned and how Cyn would react to it. 'Molly's' environmentalism would no doubt please her, but she wouldn't be too happy about the information so far on Damien Talbot. Neither was I. It was disconcerting to find myself thinking along in sync with a person I'd once been close to but had had no contact with for over two decades. It made me feel as if all the intervening years had been somehow wiped out, or at least reduced in significance. I didn't like the feeling.

Sitting there in the car, wet from the dash through the rain, and cold, I concocted two alternative hypotheses to Cyn's. One, 'Molly' had something going with Cyn's son, Geoffrey, and was checking out the mother. Two, Cyn had designed a building that had caused grief for someone connected with 'Molly' and she was following up on it. The resemblance to Eve was an irrelevance. I wasn't convinced by either theory. The first one implied that someone other than Talbot was driving the van and the second was drawing a very long bow, but they gave me a focus. Find 'Molly' and sort it out.

Tadpole Creek wasn't marked on my directory but I figured I could find it by driving around the development sites. I was wrong. Beautifully made roads led nowhere and high cyclone fences appeared without warning. I saw the completed Showgrounds, the completed State Sports Centre, the almost completed Aquatic Centre and the barely begun futuristic-looking Olympic Stadium. Car parks everywhere, vast tarmacked surfaces and five-storey cement boxes. The new railway station still managed to look like a railway station while the skeleton of a huge hotel-to-be could turn into almost anything. The Olympic Village was on a hillside overlooking the Stadium. I knew that the one they'd built for the Melbourne Olympics had turned into a low-rent public housing precinct; this one looked more likely to become a townhouse complex with its own private police force.

Eventually I pulled up in front of a half-built domed structure and waited for one of the security people to approach me. They wore blue uniforms, broad-brimmed hats and iridescent yellow rain slickers. They carried mobile phones in holsters but no guns or nightsticks that I could see.

'Yes, sir. Can I help you?'

Water dripped from the brim of her hat but she was too well-trained to pay it any attention.

'I hope so. Can you tell me where Tadpole Creek is?'

With a smooth movement she produced a map

39

and handed it to me. 'Everything of interest is marked on this map, sir. Along with information about access and so on.'

'Does it show Tadpole Creek?'

From her reaction to the question I could tell that she'd never looked at the map. I examined it. No creek.

'I'm looking for a picket line. A sort of protest site. They're against what's happening to this creek, apparently.'

She whipped out her mobile phone. 'If you'd just wait here a moment, sir, I'll find someone who can help you.'

Fair enough, I thought. *Good service*. I switched off and waited. Within a few minutes two large men appeared. One wore a suit under his raincoat rather than a uniform. He mustered up a friendly tone at odds with his expression. 'Would you care to step into the shelter, sir.'

'Look, I only wanted to know . . .'

The other guy opened the door in a manner that suggested he might try to pull me into the shelter if I elected not to step. You're at a complete physical disadvantage sitting in a car. It's much easier to hit down than to hit up. If the engine had been on I might have given them a bit of start by reversing, but it wasn't. The only advantage I had was that I wasn't standing in the rain. Then I noticed that the rain had stopped. I got out of the car.

'This way,' the suit said.

The uniform fell in behind me and we splashed through puddles to the pre-fab office. There were no chairs so we stood in the small space like people waiting for a lift to ascend.

'I'm Mr Smith . . .,' the suit began.

'Oh, good,' I said. 'Then this'll be Mr Wesson.'

They both looked at me blankly. 'No, he's . . .' It hit him then and he looked annoyed. 'Please wait outside,' he said to the other man, who went out.

'A joke,' I said.

'Yes, very funny. Now I understand you're making enquiries about the protesters.'

'Not exactly. I just wanted to know where they were.'

'Why?'

'I don't think that's any of your business.'

'And what exactly is *your* business?'

That was enough for me. I didn't like him or his style. I turned and walked out of the office. Smith shouted something and the other man moved to block my path. But I wasn't at a disadvantage now. I baulked him off balance and gave him a shove that sent him sprawling. He fell hard and rolled so that he got a lot of mud on his uniform.

'Should've kept your coat on,' I said.

He was about thirty and in pretty good shape. He came up fast in a martial arts stance that looked dangerous. I scooped up a handful of mud and threw it into his face. He bellowed and came on but he was easy meat. I tripped him and he went down again, flailing. His hands hit the edge of the paved surface. Skin was scraped and blood flowed.

41

'That's enough!' Smith shouted. A couple of other security people had gathered, but they were 'you turn right and then left' types and weren't up to coping with mud and blood. They fell back as Smith advanced.

'I've got your registration number.'

'Good.' I moved closer to him and took hold of his left hand in my right and bent it back. Since working in the gym I've acquired a fair bit of wrist and hand strength and I gave Smith the benefit of it as I moved him towards my car. I smiled at the puzzled security people. If you do this right, it can look like an intense chat between close friends.

'Where are the protesters?' I said, increasing the pressure.

'This is assault,' he ground out between clenched teeth.

'Won't show and your bloke made the first move. Where?'

'Near the railway station. Concord West.'

I released him, brushing my muddy hand on his sleeve. 'Thank you. I won't tell if you won't.'

I gave him a nod, got back in the car and reversed out. Smith shooed the onlookers away as the guy with the mud on him examined his dirty uniform and grazed hands. I never did find out his real name.

I was puzzled. I'd never heard of the Tadpole Creek protest, yet the security people treated it as a big deal. Maybe Annette was right that it had been hushed up, but that's hard to do in this day and age. More than likely it had to do with me not watching television much and switching off when I saw the word 'Olympic' in the newspaper. As a sports fan I suppose I should be enthusiastic about the Olympics and I imagine it'll suck me in when it happens. For now, I hate the hype that ignores the kids and concentrates on the millionaires running around and jumping over McDonald's and Coca-Cola signs. I might go to the boxing — I'll bet none of them are millionaires.

The sky was clearing as I drove along those new roads with the trucks that comprised most of the traffic. I located the railway station and drove slowly west back towards the Olympic site. Just past the Bicentennial Park, on the left, a road in the process of construction seemed more than usually cluttered with vehicles and equipment. I turned into it and drove less than a hundred metres before I was stopped by a row of witches' hats. The grading of the road finished here and the machines were pulled to the side. I got out and walked to where two knots of people were confronting each other on opposite sides of a creek about four metres wide. I recognised the spot from the photograph on the leaflet — same narrow stream, same scrubby trees and mangroves.

On my side were hard hats, yellow raincoats and a couple of suits, plus a pre-fab security shelter and porta-loo. On the other, jeans, bomber jackets with green stripes on the sleeves, long hair, a tent and several battered 4WDs. No psychedelic van. A banner strung between two trees read SAVE TADPOLE CREEK. A heated discussion was going on between a man in a suit a la Mr

Smith, and a tall, bearded youth who was waving a sheet of paper. I moved off to one side and went down the gentle slope, hoping to get close enough to hear what was going on without being observed. A stiff, cold wind had replaced the rain and was blowing the sounds away from me. I heard 'injunction' and 'obstruction' being shouted, cheers and jeers and not much else.

Suddenly, a hard hat spotted me.

'Media!' he shouted.

The group turned as one and, as if to relieve their frustration, four or five of them started to run towards me. I'd had enough of confronting people for one day. Without thinking I lengthened my stride, got my balance and jumped the creek.

I made it, just, and managed to keep my balance on the other side. A cheer went up from the protesters and my would-be attackers stopped dead on their side of the creek. The protesters gathered around me. I was slapped on the back. A soft drink can was shoved into my hands.

'On you, mate!'

'Great jump!'

'Let's see you do that, you pricks!'

They crowded around me, shook my hand and estimated the jump at six or seven metres. I nodded modestly although I knew differently. I was steered back to the tent. I'd slightly jarred my landing foot but I couldn't let on. As we went they jeered at the opposition on the other bank and shouted some pretty strong abuse. Some of it was very provocative and the hard hats looked provoked, but they stayed on their side. I was surprised that such a small barrier stood for so much, but I guess waterways have done that from the beginning of time.

I considered passing myself off as a representative of the media but quickly gave up the idea as unworkable. Amid all their hilarity and chatter one thing came through strongly and it was something I'd observed on other picket lines. The biggest threat to enthusiasm and commitment is boredom. My dramatic arrival had combined with their confrontation to provide a welcome break from the boredom.

We reached the tent. It was well set up with an urn, a microwave oven, a primus stove, sleeping bags. There were books and magazines in boxes and cartons containing tinned food. These people were here for the long haul. The bearded one who'd been waving the paper at the others across the water hadn't taken part in the general celebration. He was still outside the tent watching the opposition withdraw. He swung on his heel and came inside. People moved to let him through. He was in his early twenties, tall and well built with a beard like Ned Kelly.

'Ramsay Hewitt,' he said. 'And you are . . . ?'

I decided to play it straight, or straightish. He looked shrewd and for all his youth experienced, difficult to fool. 'Cliff Hardy,' I said. I put the can down and pulled the leaflet from my jacket pocket 'I came across this in the course of my work and was curious.'

'That jump of yours broke the ice, if you see

what I mean,' one of the protesters said. 'They've shoved off.'

'Shut up!' Hewitt smoothed out the leaflet as if it was a cheque in his favour that had got crumpled. 'Are you with the media?'

I was tempted to snow him for his arrogance but thought better of it. 'No. I'm a private enquiry agent.' I produced my licence but he scarcely looked at it.

'Another fascist,' he spat.

'I don't know,' I said. 'I'm opposed to the third runway. I think.'

A woman in the group laughed but as a whole they were losing interest. Hewitt turned on his heel again. He was good at that. 'Piss off.'

That suited me, more or less. I shrugged and put the leaflet and my licence folder away. 'The thing is,' I said, 'how'm I going to get back over this creek? I hurt my ankle.'

Hewitt swung back and looked as if he wanted to hit me, but he was smart enough not to. 'Look,' he said. 'It doesn't surprise me that the security service here've set up someone like you to do something fucking flash and infiltrate us. A good long jump. So what? It's an old trick. It happened . . .'

'At the siege of Chicago,' I said. 'Yeah, I've read the Mailer book too.'

'You make my point. Bugger off.'

'I'd like to ask a few questions.'

'Don't push your luck. No-one here'll talk to you.'

'You speak for everyone, do you? Who's the fascist now?'

He walked away. It seemed to be coffee time and the other protesters were milling round the urn and the microwave, except for a woman who was watching me from a distance. For no good reason I formed the impression that she was the one who'd laughed at my third runway reference. I moved away slightly and she followed. She kept an eye on Hewitt until she saw he was fully occupied in discussion over his precious piece of paper. She approached me with her hand out.

'I'm Tess Hewitt, Ramsay's sister. Don't mind him, he's on edge.'

She was in her thirties, tall and athletic-looking in jeans and a denim jacket. She had short blonde hair, brown eyes and regular features. A slight over-bite. Her handshake was firm.

'He's too suspicious,' I said. 'I'm not what he said.'

'Then what're you doing here?'

I took out the photograph of Eve and showed it to her. 'A missing persons case. Do you know this woman? Or someone who looks like her?'

She glanced at the photo and bit her lip. 'Of course I do. That's Meg French, the poor thing.'

47

6

Her remark jolted me. 'Why?' I said, 'What's the matter with her?'

I must have spoken more urgently than I'd intended because she looked at me closely. 'Now I see it. The slight resemblance. Is there a family connection?'

'Could be. It's a long story. But why did you call her a poor thing?'

She reached out and touched my arm. 'I was referring to that dreadful boyfriend of hers, Damien. He's violent and dishonest. I don't know what she sees in him.'

'I've been told he's good-looking.'

'Oh, yes. Certainly he's that. And bags of charm. He comes across as bright, but I suspect he really isn't.'

Generally speaking, I don't like being touched by strangers, but I didn't mind at all in her case. There was a warmth about her that was welcome and I was in need of some human comfort. 'You say he's violent. Towards her?'

'I saw him hit her once, yes.'

'Jesus.'

'The funny thing is, it was after she did what you just did.'

I was confused. 'What?'

'She jumped the creek. Just for fun. She cleared it by a bit more than you though.'

'It's not such a great jump. Twelve or thirteen feet.'

'It's not bad in jeans and boots or dressed like you and from a soft take-off.'

'He hit her?'

'For showing off. Understandable in a way. He's — what would you say — mildly disabled. One leg shorter than the other. He wears a built-up boot.'

'Look, Tess, this is all very important. Can we go somewhere for a talk?'

'No. There'll be a meeting in a few minutes to plan the next phase. I have to be at it. Ramsay hopes to get his idea through while Damien's not here. They're sort of rivals.'

I had questions — why did it matter whether Talbot was there or not; how had Meg French reacted to being hit, and where were she and Talbot now? I settled for the most important. 'Do you know where Talbot and . . . Meg are now?'

'No, but they'll be back. My impression is that they live in that van most of the time. But I have a feeling they also have a place somewhere. A squat or something.'

I shook my head. I didn't fancy relaying too much of this to Cyn. I asked her where this might be and she said she didn't know.

'He changes the paint job on the van from time to time. Sometimes it's plain, then it's all sorts of colours. I think that's illegal. I asked him about it. He calls it urban guerilla tactics.'

Great, I thought. *That'll make it tougher.* 'I really need to get hold of them,' I said. 'It's not about your protest in any way. I — '

She touched me again and I had the same reaction. 'I understand,' she said. 'Look, they'll be back. Give me your phone number and I'll do what I can to help you. That's on one condition.'

I was fishing for a card before she finished. 'Good. What's that?'

'That you tell me about this long story of yours sometime.' She took the card. 'Thanks. I have to go.'

She moved back towards the tent and I walked along the bank of the creek looking for an easier place to cross. I found it less than a hundred metres away where the creek entered a concrete channel crossed by a narrow bridge. Upstream from that it disappeared into a pipe. I stood on the bridge looking back. The creek was exposed for not much more than two hundred metres. The mangroves seemed to be just clinging on against the pollution and the development. The whole thing looked like an oversight, as if such a feeble watercourse should have been covered long ago and the patch of marshland where it ended drained. I wondered what the rationale for protecting it was. It wasn't an attractive feature, but in a way I could see why it was worth preserving whether or not animal or vegetable species were threatened. With the whole of the landscape being restructured, why not say hands off this little bit?

My car was standing where I'd left it and there was no-one around. The machines that would cover the creek and build the road had withdrawn to other parts of the site. It looked as if this represented no more than a stay in the proceedings, but you never know, we've still got Victoria Street and Fraser Island.

The rain started again as I drove home and the going was slow. I debated whether to call Cyn and tell her what I'd learned but I decided against. None of it was comforting and perhaps if I found out a bit more I could put a better complexion on things. I realised I was hoping for the same thing for myself. I wasn't too displeased with my progress so far — to identify an unknown person and establish a connection that could lead to making contact wasn't such a bad day's work. It was certainly worth a drink or two and I was looking forward to it. The fact that I'd be having the drink alone made me think briefly of Annette and then, for somewhat longer, of Tess Hewitt.

Back when Bob Hawke was ruling the roost, there was a proposal that all Australians should be issued with an identity card to be called the Australia Card. The idea was that the card would make it easier for the authorities to catch up with tax cheats, welfare frauds and other fiddlers with the system. The outcry against it came from the left and the right and the proposal was scuttled. I was against it instinctively as a sort of crypto-anarchist and a reader of George Orwell. Big Brother didn't need any more of a leg-up. Civil libertarians spelled out how it would've violated privacy in the affairs of the citizens from sexual preference to political affiliation and back again. As it turned out, they were right and they were wrong. These days, if you know how, you can find out just about anything about anybody if you can tap into the vast computerised data banks held by government agencies, financial and educational institutions and the free-wheeling marketplace.

I drove to my office in Darlinghurst, ignored the mail and the faxes, and made a series of phone calls. Pressing all the right buttons is costly, but if you've got a name and a birthdate, not to mention extra information like a mother's maiden name, it's astonishing what's on record and how easily freelance hackers can access, assemble and market it. Everyone in my business is a subscriber to one or more of these services. You pay off in lots of different ways — depositing in TAB accounts, permitting items to be debited to your account in various stores and outlets, providing services free, doing favours. It's dirty, but it's essential to survival in the modern inquirer business.

When I'd finished I tidied up the paperwork, made a few calls to keep other cases ticking over and declared my unavailability to two would-be clients I'd normally have gobbled up. I spread Cyn's cheque out on the desk and debated whether to deposit it. What kind of a bastard would take money from a dying woman to locate and protect his own daughter? On the other hand, what professional would devote time and resources to chasing a fantasy? So far, the pursuit of Damien Talbot and Meg (aka Margaret? Megan?) French had cost time and petrol, lost me some business and the bills from the hackers would come in. Cyn's cheque would cover it but there wouldn't be a lot over.

It was after five and the rain was washing the windows — the only way they ever got washed. I'd bought a bottle of Teacher's on the way in. I opened it, poured a good measure into a paper cup and put my feet on the desk. The ankle I'd jarred making my famous jump twinged and I grimaced as I swallowed some medicinal Scotch. The most I'd ever cleared in the broad jump at school was a bit over sixteen feet which placed me third in the Sydney inter-school athletic car-nival. That recollection brought back a memory of who'd won it — a pale, orange-haired, stocky kid named 'Redda' Phillips from Fort Street High. He'd also won the hop-step-and-jump, the high jump and the two sprints. It was a privilege to be beaten by him. I had another drink and wondered if kids still called redheads 'Redda' or 'Bluey'. Somehow I doubted it.

I knew what I was doing — putting off calling Cyn. I folded the cheque and put it into my wallet. Indecisive. That wasn't me. I picked up the phone, dialled and got her answering machine. I left a message that I was making progress but had nothing solid yet. The easy way out. I took the bottle home with me.

7

At 9.30 the next morning I answered the phone to a solicitor named Hargreaves who told me that unless I presented at his office by 11 o'clock that morning for a conference with representatives of Millennium Security I could expect extremely unpleasant legal proceedings. Assault was mentioned, along with trespass and damage to property. I couldn't afford to get involved in anything like that so I agreed.

The office was in Macquarie Street in a section of the city that wasn't being torn down. I wore a suit. Mr Hargreaves wore a suit. So did Mr Hargreaves's female secretary and Smith from Millennium. The other person present wore the Millennium Security guard uniform. He wasn't the one who'd fallen in the puddle. This guy was bigger and well-balanced, looked harder to trip.

'Mr Hardy,' Smith said. 'I think you remember me. This is Mr Kamenka. Thank you for coming. A few minutes of your time could save a lot of wasted time for all of us.'

'Time is money,' I said.

'Indeed it is.' Hargreaves gestured for us all to sit down.

Smith opened the slimline leather satchel he was carrying and extracted a manilla folder which he placed on the solicitor's teak desk.

'This is a complete rundown of all the steps that have been taken to protect the Homebush Bay environment,' he said. 'It includes details of detoxification, the rehabilitation of wetlands, the restitution of original watercourses, the isolation of noxious wastes, the retention of existing trees and the re-planting of appropriate species, the installation of solar-powered heating and lighting systems and . . .'

'Fascinating reading I'm sure,' I interrupted. 'But what's it got to do with me?'

'Yesterday you made an enquiry at the site, following which you assaulted a member of our staff and later appeared to make common cause with the picketers at Tadpole Creek.'

I looked at Kamenka. 'It wasn't much of an assault. More of a nudge.'

'Certainly actionable if we chose to make it so.'

'Ah, a threat.'

'No. Just a piece of information to go along with this.' He tapped the folder. 'Read it, Mr Hardy. I don't know what ratbag organisation you're working for, but frustrating the work at the site is ill-advised and pointless.'

'You call that whole thing the site, do you? Isn't it a whole lot of sites?'

Smith was struggling to keep his patience.

'We're trying to treat you decently. Don't make it any harder.'

'What puzzles me is why you're so worried and why you're taking this trouble. I don't give a stuff about Tadpole Creek. I don't care about the Olympics either, although if you could give me some tickets to the boxing I might be interested. Can Mr Kamenka speak, by the way? Or does he just do isometrics inside his uniform?'

Smith sighed and Hargreaves looked exasperated. I didn't blame him. I was exasperated too. The secretary entered with coffee and we all watched her pour it.

I sipped the coffee. Too strong, bitter.

Smith's manners were his strong point. He backed down a little, talked about some of the hassles he had with security and implied that he was under some pressure to keep the lid on all difficult situations. His politeness seemed genuine and made me feel better about him. I decided to give a little.

'I'm working on a missing persons case. That's all I can tell you and more than I need to tell you. There's nothing more to it than that.'

'I'd like to believe you.'

I put the undrunk coffee on the desk. 'You can.'

'If that's the case I might have a proposition for you.'

'I enter into contracts with clients, Mr Smith. Just like you. I don't deal in propositions.'

Smith considered this carefully before nodding. 'I see. Well, just let me lay this out for you and get your reaction.'

Pointedly, I checked my watch.

'This won't take long,' he said. He explained that the Tadpole Creek protest was a puzzle to the Olympic organising authorities and particularly to Millennium Security. He described the creek as 'a puddle' of no environmental value, although he admitted that it was an oversight that it hadn't been included in the original environmentally-sensitive plan.

'I won't pretend this has been well-handled,' he said. 'When they saw that they'd slipped it up they tried to tidy things away sharpish. Crudely. This protest surfaced and we're in the spot we're in now. Somehow they got some mad judge to issue an injunction. It's crazy.'

'Look, I'm not really interested. I . . .'

'There's someone behind it,' Smith continued. 'Someone with money. That protest is being funded from somewhere. Food, equipment, vehicles, legal fees. Someone's backing the whole thing and we don't know who or why.'

I shrugged. 'You must have the resources to find out.'

'The way to find out is to get someone inside the protest. It seems you made a big hit with them.' He opened his satchel and took out a notebook. 'I'm told you had a long conversation with the sister of one of the leaders. That's Tess Hewitt, sister of Ramsay. This is after you jumped the creek.'

For my own reasons, I was interested now. 'Who's the other leader?'

Smith didn't need to consult his notes. 'Damien Talbot. He's a sort of environmental terrorist —

57

the kind who drives spikes into logging trees. That kind of thing. He's also got convictions for drug offences and criminal assault.'

Just for a minute I was tempted. I'd heard of Millennium. They were international, of course, wielded influence and paid top money. But I smelt several rats. The theory that I was well-placed to infiltrate the protesters was only half-convincing at best. Millennium should've been able to come up with better strategies that that. Then there was Tess Hewitt and the warmth I'd felt from her. Not to be discounted. Also, I'd begun to focus in on the Meg French matter with all its emotional complications and I work best when I'm single-minded. Double-minded maybe. Triple-minded, never.

'I'm sorry,' I said. 'I've got something serious in hand and the protest is very peripheral to it. If that. I'm not interested.'

'If it's a question of money?'

'No.'

Smith sighed and put his notebook away. 'Then all I can do is advise you to do as you say — leave those idiots to their fate.'

I had to admire Hargreaves and Kamenka. Neither had said a word. Now both stood in mute and effective demonstration that the meeting was over. I stayed where I was.

'A threat of legal action brought me here, Mr Smith.'

Smith had half-left his seat. Now he stood and moved towards the door. 'Hardly a threat and I think we've resolved the issue.'

'I like a quiet life, too,' I said.

'Do you? I doubt it.'

And that was that. On consideration, Smith impressed me as an honest functionary. Maybe there *was* a mystery about the backer of the protest. Maybe I could ask Tess Hewitt about it.

The information began to come in soon after I reached my office. Damien Talbot was twenty-six years of age. Born in Petersham, he had suffered a childhood accident that had left his right leg slightly shorter than his left. He wore a built-up boot but walked with a limp. He was 185 centimetres and 75 kilos with fair hair, blue eyes and pierced ears. He had attended state schools in inner Sydney and done one year of an acting course at NIDA then dropped out. Some time later he'd enrolled in a TAFE Environmental Studies course which he'd pursued for two years without completing the required written work. Addresses in Ultimo, Chippendale, Newtown, Marrickville and of course Homebush. He had two convictions for possession of marijuana and one for trafficking in cocaine. He'd served three years on that count, concurrent with a two-year sentence for assault occasioning bodily harm. That was all to do with drugs too.

His driver's licence had expired a year ago and, as I'd already learned, he was being proceeded against for failure to pay parking fines and for driving an unroadworthy vehicle. He had drawn unemployment benefits periodically but was not currently doing so. I obtained an address for his surviving parent, his mother, in Petersham and details of three bank accounts, all overdrawn. It was difficult to find much on the credit side of Damien's ledger.

Megan Sarah French had been born in Bathurst at St Margaret's Hospital twenty-three years ago. Her birth date was given as one day after the date Cyn claimed to have had her child. Her adoptive parents were Rex and Dora French of Katoomba. Megan Sarah French had attended the St Josephine Convent in Katoomba. She was a prefect, leader of the debating team and captain of the netball squad that won the country division championship in her final year. She scored 90.5 in the HSC and matriculated at the University of New South Wales. She'd dropped out of a degree course in industrial relations after two years.

I jotted the information down from the phone calls and arranged the faxes in order as they came in. I drank the whole of a pot of strong coffee and made another as things began to sink in. The confirmation of Cyn's story seemed to be staring me in the face and I found it hard to adjust to. I'd been hoping, or at least half-hoping, for something to blow the whole idea out of the water, but all I was getting were blocks building towards the same conclusion.

The data continued to flow. Megan Sarah had enrolled in the same TAFE Environmental Studies course as Talbot and had dropped out at the same time. *Connection*. She'd drawn unemployment benefits at various times and signed on for several re-training programs without completing them. *Not good*. A couple of credit cards had been withdrawn for failure to meet payments. No prosecutions. She held a driver's licence but no vehicle was registered in her name. She had never lost any points on her licence, and there was nothing outstanding. No criminal convictions.

It was ambiguous stuff to convey to Cyn and I resolved to edit it. I got the suit wet walking in the rain to the Post Office to consult the Blue Mountains telephone directory. There were three entries for French and one with the initial R. Back in the office, with the suit jacket on a hanger, I rang the most likely number and drew a blank — R was for Robert and he had no knowledge of a Rex. Ditto with the next. The third French was Rex's brother, Frank, and he was happy to talk to me when I told him I was a private detective.

'Is the prick in trouble?' he said.

'No, I want to talk to him about his daughter, Megan. She's . . . ah, missing.'

'That poor kid.'

This was the second time that expression had been used. 'Why d'you say that, Mr French?'

'Rex and Dora are religious fanatics. First it was Catholicism, strict as buggery. Megan was supposed to be a nun. They tried to beat God into her, made her life a misery and she was a super kid. When she kicked over the traces, wanted to go to university and that, they went nuts.'

'What did they do to her?'

'Kicked her out. Then they sold everything they had and joined a bloody cult up here. They get around praying and scratching in the dirt.'

'I'd like to talk to them.'

'You'll have to come up then. There's no phone out there.'

He gave me directions to a five-hectare property near Mount Wilson operated by the Society for Harmony and Tranquility.

I thanked him. 'Do you think they'd be in touch with Megan?'

'Rex? No way. Dora might be. She's under his thumb but she not quite as crazy as he is. Tell him Frank sent you. That'll really get up his nose.'

8

It wasn't a day for the mountains. Sydney was cool and wet, the mountains were likely to be cooler and possibly wetter. I grabbed a parka I keep in the office and headed west. Mentally, I picked through the information I'd acquired about Megan and Talbot. It could be structured not to sound too bad — a 'crazy mixed-up kids' gloss could be put on it. But it could be a lot worse in reality, with the drugs and Talbot's violence factored in. I tried to treat it like any missing persons case — concerned parent, worrying features, bad associations — but the personal aspect kept cutting in, confusing me and making me unsure of my assessments.

The country around Mount Wilson looked bleak in the pale winter light. After a long, hot summer there hadn't been much rain until recently and the land was parched-looking and damply yellow. Frank French's directions were good and I located the property easily. It was at the end of a long dirt road and the word that sprang to mind to describe it was neglect. The fences were in poor repair, broken down in spots by the press of branches, sagging elsewhere from wood rot. The driveway to the main building had once been covered with gravel but now the rocky ground was showing through. The rambling main building, constructed from what looked like rough, pit-sawn local timber, immediately struck me as odd. It was huddled down amid trees and shrubs in a hollow as if deliberately trying to avoid the view to the west. If it had been located just a few metres in that direction on higher ground it would have commanded a magnificent outlook over paddocks to forest and far ranges.

The garden beds and lawn flanking the driveway were scruffy. An old Land Rover was parked on a patch of remaining gravel to the left near a rusting pre-fab shed. I stopped dead in front of the building, got out and looked around. No telephone lines, no electricity cables, no TV antenna. Isolation. The right context for dogma and obedience. The place depressed me already.

I suppose I expected white robes and sandals, but the man who met me at the top of the front steps wore a business suit and a business-like expression.

'Welcome to Harmony and Tranquility,' he said. 'How may I help you?'

He was middle-aged, plump, balding, normal-looking, so I behaved normally by showing him my PEA licence and telling him that I wanted to talk to Rex and Dora French on a family matter. I'd put the parka on in the car to keep myself dry on the dash to the building. I took it off and revealed myself in suit and tie. No gun bulge. No knuckle-duster.

'I believe they're both meditating. Nothing distressing I hope?'

I made a non-committal gesture which he didn't like and he liked it still less when I asked him who he was.

'Pastor John,' he said. 'The leader of this community. I'll make enquiries about Brother Rex and Sister Dora. If you'll just wait inside?'

He ushered me up the steps and through the door into a room on the left. I had time to glimpse a faded carpet in the hallway, a lack of light, and to smell a musty odour that confirmed my impression of neglect. The room I stood in was bare apart from an old set of church pews arranged around three sides. The window was small and the panes were dusty, inside and out.

After a few minutes a woman came into the room. She was fiftyish, small and tired-looking. Her grey hair was wispy and the cardigan she wore over a woollen dress was ill-buttoned. No make-up, thick stockings, flat-heeled shoes. She stopped one step into the room and looked at me as if I was going to bite her.

'Yes?'

'Mrs French?'

'Yes.'

I went into a quick explanation, fearing that Rex couldn't be far away. At the mention of Megan's name she sparked up.

'Oh, oh,' she said. 'It's been so long. How is she?'

'I don't know, Mrs French. I'm trying to find her. You love her?'

'Oh, yes. Megan is wonderful. The best thing in my life. But Rex . . .'

'Her natural mother is dying and wants to see her.'

Her thin, blue-veined hands flew up to her face, almost hiding it. This was too much hard-edged information for her to process. She dropped the hands and looked up at me. 'The poor woman.'

'Yes. Do you know where Megan might be, Mrs French? People seem to think she might have a place to go to.'

'People?'

'People who care for her. People who want to help her. She's keeping bad company, Mrs French.'

I could hear some sort of movement inside the house. Rex? I whipped out a card and extended it. She didn't move and I had to grab one of her hands and wrap it around the card. She clutched it like a child with a toy. I asked her again where Megan might go but she'd heard the sounds herself by now and didn't reply.

The man who entered the room was big and bulky. He was fair, a redhead who'd turned grey I guessed. His pale skin was blotched with freckles and whitish skin cancers. He towered over his wife and almost shouldered her aside to confront me.

'You are?'

I told him.

'Your business?'

I told him.

He sensed that his wife was moving so as to be

66

able to look at me and he pushed her towards the door. 'I'll handle this, Dora.'

She shot me a quick, hopeless look and left the room.

'Megan's mother was a whore,' Rex French said. 'Like mother, like child.'

It took every atom of self-control I had in me not to hit him. 'That's not a very Christian attitude,' I said.

'The word is be-fouled by your use of it.'

He was sixty or thereabouts, flabby and slack-bodied in overalls and work boots. A decent punch would destroy him but I'd met enough fanatics to know how useless it is to argue with or assault them.

'You're pathetic,' I said. 'She deserved something better than you.'

'Leave!'

I had to clench my fists to control the impulse to plant one in that soft belly. 'I'm going. By the way, your brother Frank doesn't say hello.'

French snorted. 'Another sinner.'

'No, a human being. Not a sack of self-righteous shit like you.'

'How dare you,' he shouted.

Pastor John and two other men entered the room. They looked at me as if I'd shat on the carpet.

'I'm afraid you've upset Brother Rex,' Pastor John said. 'I must ask you to leave before you create more disharmony.'

They represented no physical threat but I was repelled by their self-righteous disapproval. I drove away feeling sorry for Megan who'd spent something like sixteen years with Rex French, sorry for his wife, sorry for Cyn and sorry for myself. Sorry.

9

'Cultists!' Cyn almost screamed at me. 'What do you mean cultists?'

'Apparently they were Catholics . . .'

'That's nearly as bad.'

Religion, dislike of it, was one of the few attitudes Cyn and I had had in common and nothing had changed.

We were sitting in the living room of Cyn's flat. Contrary to what she'd told me, there were no signs of medication and illness. The flat was elegant, as I would've expected. Elegant, but not obsessively so. Cyn had always had good taste and had only let it slip once — when she'd married me. I couldn't identify the pictures on the walls or tell who'd designed the furniture, but I knew someone had. I can't tell a leather couch from a vinyl one on sight either, but I was sure what I was sitting on was the real hide. I'd thought it was better to talk face to face with Cyn about what I learned so I'd driven straight to Crows Nest from the mountains. Now I wasn't so sure. She was working herself up into a fury as she used to do when we were together and I'd transgressed.

She paced the room with energy she'd summoned up from somewhere. 'Cultists. What sort of a life must she have led? They're insane, they have group sex. They . . .'

'Cyn, shut up! We'll talk about this rationally or I'll leave and phone that son of yours and get him to come over and take care of you.'

'You don't know his number.'

'You think not?'

'God, you're a bastard.'

'When I have to be. Why doesn't your daughter come around? And you never talk about her.'

Cyn sat down in one of the leather chairs and all the energy left her in a rush. 'We've fallen out, Anne and I. It's nothing serious.'

I had my doubts about that and I wondered whether the falling out had contributed to the search for the lost child. I was out of my depth. 'Look,' I said. 'The place of birth checks out. The date's one day out, though. I suppose this Megan French could be your daughter.'

'*Our* daughter.'

I'd told Cyn about Meg French's early academic record and about her jump across the creek. I hadn't mentioned Talbot hitting her. 'She's athletic and bright . . .'

'And running around with some low-life. That's you coming out in her.'

'Cyn.'

She covered her face with her hands. Her hair flopped forward and suddenly, thin and frail in a silk dress that was loose on her, she looked old. She lifted her face and pushed back the hair. 'I'm sorry, Cliff. I'm sorry. It's late in the day. Would you like a drink?'

'I would. If you'll have one.'

'I hardly slept at all last night. On all these pills sometimes you do and sometimes you don't. It feels bloody late in the day to me. I generally have a brandy at seven o'clock when I watch the news. I think I'll have one now. You?'

'Why not?'

She went to the kitchen for ice and soda water and poured the brandy from a decanter on a shelf. The tray also held bottles of gin and Scotch — I would've preferred either of them, but what the hell.

'Cheers,' she said. We touched glasses. 'D'you remember when we used to like brandy, lime and soda? I wonder if people still drink that these days?'

'Haven't heard of it lately,' I said. 'It wasn't a bad drink though.' I sipped. 'This is pretty smooth.'

But from the way she set it down on the arm of the chair I could tell that she wasn't really interested in the alcohol. 'So what's your next move? It doesn't sound as if you pushed very hard up there. They must know where she'd go.'

I was enjoying the drink. *Brandy at 6.30*, I thought. *Have to watch out for that.* 'I don't think so. The woman does possibly, but the husband's got her hog-tied. You have to watch your step these days. Can't throw your weight around like before. She'll turn up again at this environmental thing.'

She gestured impatiently, almost upsetting her glass. 'So we just wait? That doesn't sound like the old Cliff. Goes with the suit, does it?'

I sipped the smooth brandy and didn't say anything.

'French,' Cyn mused. 'Quite a nice name for such nasty people. You said that her ... uncle I suppose we have to call him, spoke well of her?'

'Everything speaks well of her, Cyn, except her association with this Talbot. But for that, I wouldn't be too worried.'

'Wouldn't you? But that's you all over, isn't it? Not worrying about other people. Well, he went to NIDA. What does that say about him?'

I let her waspishness pass. 'I don't know anything about NIDA except they train actors there. Didn't Mel Gibson go there?'

'Dropped out I think, like this one. That's another thing I don't like — this dropping out. Jesus, Cliff, how're you going to *find* her? You can't just wait for her to turn up.'

'I'll keep looking. That's all I can do. I'll talk to people at these schools they've gone to. Try to squeeze something out.'

Cyn took a long swallow of her drink. 'Yes, of course. You have to find her. You have to talk to your daughter.'

And you probably need to talk to yours, I thought but didn't say. I just nodded.

Cyn's eyes narrowed and at first I thought she was experiencing some deep pain, but it was a gesture of concentration, penetration. 'You *know* she's yours, don't you, Cliff?'

I took a drink. 'I was a dropout, too,' I said.

Cyn smiled and the fatigue and fragility momentarily fell away. 'So you were, and you didn't turn out so badly.'

I left, promising to keep in close touch and tell her everything I learned even though I'd already glossed over many things, particularly about Talbot, and I didn't plan to change. She thanked me and reminded me again of my stake in the matter. For no good reason, the thought of DNA testing came into my head and I recoiled from it. She didn't mention the cheque and neither did I.

10

I spent the next morning working hard and not getting far. I spoke on the phone to a NIDA lecturer who remembered Talbot.

'He thought of himself as a method actor,' he said. 'And he thought that just meant being his normal, charming, conceited self. He was wrong and he didn't like it when he found out.'

Through a contact in the Corrective Services Department I tried to get information on Talbot's prison record and failed. I went to the TAFE college in North Sydney where both Talbot and Megan had studied and drew a blank with Talbot. No-one remembered him. But Dr Sylvia Davis, who taught something called environmental philosophy, remembered Megan.

'Very bright,' she said. 'Her first semester results were HD.'

'Sorry, that means?'

'High Distinction. First class honours in the old style.'

The college, with its multiple acronyms, codes and facilities like condom-vending machines in the toilets, had made me feel very old style. I asked what had happened to Megan subsequently.

Dr Davis didn't even have to consult a file. 'She dropped out. Didn't submit an exercise, didn't turn up for her seminar presentation. That's the worst sign.'

'Did you try to find out why?'

She sighed and looked around her tiny office, cluttered with books, folders and video cassettes. 'Mr Hardy, have you any idea of what my work load here is like? You were lucky, you caught me with fifteen minutes to spare. Look, I wrote a note to the address we had on file. It came back stamped "not-known-at-this-address". That's all I could do. I'm sorry. I hope you can find her. She had great potential.'

No comfort, that. I went to my car and sat thinking, working out the best way to tackle Talbot's mother. The mobile rang.

'Mr Hardy? This is Tess Hewitt. I've been trying to get you for an hour or more. Why don't you answer your mobile?'

'I don't carry the phone with me. Can't stand it. Have they shown up? Are they there now?'

'Been and gone,' she said. 'I think you should get over here. A man's been killed.'

'Killed? What man? Who by?'

'They say Damien Talbot did it. He and Meg were here, now they've gone.'

'Jesus. Right, I'm on my way.'

'No, on second thoughts, don't come here. There's police all over the place and I'm going to be flat out keeping Ramsay calm. I just snuck off to let you know.'

'Did she go with Talbot willingly?'

'Look, I can't talk now. We'll have to meet later.'

There was sense in what she was saying and I fought down my impatience. 'Okay. Where and when?'

'Come to my place this afternoon. Say about three. The police should be finished with us by then.'

She gave me an address in Concord and rang off. I dropped the phone on the passenger seat and stared through the windscreen. The rain of the past few days had cleared and the day was fine and still. The water and wind had removed the pollution and I could see the whole length of the tree-lined street. I could see the arch of the bridge above the building line. Things were changing here too. They were knocking things down and throwing things up in search of the dollar but at least it wasn't the Olympic tourist dollar. Just for once, the north side of the city had more appeal for me than the south.

On the drive south I caught a news broadcast that gave the usual sparse details on the events at Tadpole Creek. No names were mentioned and the writer of the bulletin obviously had almost no knowledge about the picket line. A man had been killed and police were investigating and that was about it.

I was worried, but I tried to adopt a professional attitude. I had a good source and would learn more in time. I drove to the public library in Glebe and used the Internet to dig up whatever I could on the work at Homebush. The information was vast and I printed out only the odd page. According to the official version, every effort had been made to clean up what had been dirty, restore what had been damaged and preserve everything of value. The sanctimonious tone of the material made me suspicious and I knew something the compilers didn't — that a straggly waterway named Tadpole Creek had escaped their notice.

Just to be thorough, I searched for Tadpole Creek. Slim pickings — an account of a picnic there in the 1930s attended by some minor member of the Royal family; a stormwater and drainage proposal not proceeded with after the war; an offer by a consortium to build a tennis facility involving piping of the creek, rejected by the council in the mid-eighties and a Native Title claim lodged in 1996 but withdrawn a year later due to the discovery of an unspecified mistake in old maps of the area.

Tess Hewitt's house was a Californian bungalow on a large block with the backyard abutting the golf course. The driveway held a newish Holden Barina that would have had to brush branches aside to get to where it was parked. The front lawn was badly in need of mowing and the bushes and shrubs wanted a trim. I parked behind the Barina and went along a series of cement circles to the porch. The circles were overgrown and in danger of disappearing. A large thistle poked up knee-high in front of the porch steps.

'Neglected, isn't it?' Tess Hewitt said.

I pulled up the thistle, knocked the soil from the roots and tossed it aside. 'You should see my place.'

Tess stood at the top of the steps looking down at me. She wore black ski pants, medium heels and a white silk blouse with full sleeves. She held a glass of red wine in one hand and a bottle in the other.

'You caught me red-handed.'

Despite my anxiety, I laughed and went up the steps. 'I'm glad you're all right. You seemed pretty upset on the phone. The news people don't know a thing. What's happening?'

'Come in and I'll tell you all about it. I know you've got an interest, but so have I. Ramsay. I'm resolved not to panic and I regard red wine as the best anti-panic formula in the world. Do you drink red wine?'

'I do.'

We went in. The front rooms were dim, as they often are in such houses, but the back had been opened up to the light by some tasteful renovation — a skylight, big windows, sliding glass doors. We went through to a tiled area with cane furniture and indoor plants. A low table held a loaf of sliced rye bread, fetta cheese on a board, black olives still in their delicatessen plastic bowl, some plates. Tess Hewitt had grabbed another glass on the way through the kitchen. She poured for me and topped up her own.

'I heard the car pull up,' she said. She wasn't sober exactly, but she was a long way from drunk.

'It needs a tune. Still, that's good hearing.' I raised my glass to her. 'Cheers.'

She acknowledged the gesture but didn't respond. She might not have panicked, but she was battling against something else. The food on the table reminded me that I'd skipped lunch. It must have showed because she forced a smile and picked up a knife from the cheese board. 'Hungry?'

The wine was smooth and good and would've disposed me to eat even if I hadn't been hungry. I nodded. 'Please. I missed lunch.'

'I tried to eat but I couldn't. I didn't think private detectives concerned themselves about things like lunch. You disappoint me.' She concentrated hard, frowning, as she sliced some cheese and put it on a plate with some bread and half a dozen olives and passed it to me with a paper napkin which I immediately dropped.

'I've never been able to keep one of these things where they should be,' I said. 'They usually end up on the floor.'

'Don't worry. I'm glad to have some company and see someone acting normally. I can't, quite. Have a bite and I'll tell you what happened.'

She took a good slug of wine and told me that she'd stayed at the picket line overnight, dossing down in a sleeping bag in the tent. 'I do that pretty often,' she said. 'Act as a sort of organiser and keeper-together of things. Ramsay can't do it all and there's sometimes disputes and arguments that need a subtle touch.'

I nodded. I wanted her to get to the point, but the bread and cheese and wine were hitting the spot and I was enjoying looking at her. Unprofessional, I know, but it was polite to let her tell it her way and I sensed that that in her tense, edgy state, politeness was a good strategy.

'I woke up in the early hours. I knew the noise. It was that bloody van of Damien's. It's got a shot muffler. I thought, *Good, I'll try to get Meg to stick around and I'll get through to Mr Hardy*. I went back to sleep. A bit later I woke up again and there was a scream and shouts and lights and bangings and clangs. I pulled on my pants and went out. It was just dawn and bloody cold. I heard a woman scream and I saw the van roaring off. A few people were huddled together over near the creek. There's a spot where you can cross on some rocks and a log. There was a man on the ground with his head beaten in. It was horrible. The faint light made it worse, sort of. Like in a black and white movie. The blood looked black.'

She had another drink and I finished what I was eating and left the rest on my plate. 'I know what you mean,' I said. 'I've seen it. Who was he?'

She sucked in a deep breath. 'One of the security people.'

'Jesus.'

'It was hard to work out what had happened because it was dark and there were people moving around. We mount a sort of watch at night, you see. The way it *looks* is that Damien took it on himself to scout around and found this security man on our side of the creek. There could have been a fight. I don't know. But the man's dead and Damien's gone.'

She set her glass down hard on the table. 'I know what *you* want to ask. What about Megan?

80

But think about me. The police are charging Ramsay with being an accessory or something.'

I told her that the charge of being an accessory in matters like this was largely a bluff and seldom led to any serious consequences. 'Have you got a lawyer?'

She nodded. 'Yes. We've had one all along. Bill Damelian. But he's really an environmental man. I don't think he does any criminal stuff.'

'Doesn't matter. Environmental lawyers deal with bail and all that stuff regularly. And he'll know who to talk to if it goes any further,' I said. 'Don't worry.'

She picked up her glass and looked at me. 'For some unknown bloody reason I believe you. Why would that be?'

'Experience,' I said. 'I've been around lawyers and police and crims for more than twenty years. You get a feel for where the real danger lies. Not always right about it, but . . .'

'Okay, the police took Ramsay off, but he was pretty composed and I got onto Bill. He said he'd be right on it. You're saying he'll get Ramsay out.'

I nodded. 'It mightn't go so well for the protest, though.'

She shrugged. 'You win some, you lose some.' She poured some more wine for us. 'Thanks. You're a comfort. Right. Well, Megan. She went off with Damien, I'm sorry to tell you.'

I repeated what I'd asked her on the phone. 'Willingly?'

'I can't say. I *would* say that I think the scream I heard when I woke up was hers, and that I heard

81

her scream again just before the van roared off.'

'Meaning that the first scream might have been when she saw the body, so she wasn't there when it happened, and the second one was a protest at being dragged off?'

'I hope so. For her sake and yours.' She looked at me keenly. 'I don't really know you, of course. But just at a guess I'd say you're taking this missing persons case rather personally. How come?'

I told her. Before she could respond the phone rang.

She took the call and from the few words I heard I guessed it was from the lawyer so I moved out to the back verandah to give her some privacy. The back garden bore the same hallmarks of neglect as the front. It was somehow sad. I've never lived with anyone long enough or in an appropriate place to reshape a piece of land together. Clearly, that's what had happened here once. A fishpond showed signs of heavy work — not professionally done, but satisfactorily. The flowers in the well-mulched garden beds had been carefully tended at one time; not any more.

I wandered down the overgrown path and found a screened-in vegetable garden that told the same story — crude but solid carpentry, a considerable amount of earth moved, subtle touches.

'What're you doing?'

I turned to see Tess on the verandah, shielding her eyes against the late afternoon sun. Her posture was tense, almost aggressive. I walked back, careful to avoid a rake that lay on the ground, teeth up.

'I was getting out of your way while you were on the phone. Something bad?'

She nodded. 'They're charging Ramsay as an accessory to unlawful death and opposing bail. I thought you said accessory charges didn't amount to anything.'

She was upset, looking for someone to blame. Lawyers are great at deflecting blame, I seem to have a knack for attracting it. 'It depends. What does the lawyer say?'

'He says he's working on it. Ramsay'll have to stay in custody tonight at least.'

'It won't be so bad. He — '

'Oh, he'll love it! He's been looking for it for ages. Martyrdom's just his style, the idiot.'

We went back into the house and Tess made coffee. It seemed to fit the new mood. She told me that her parents had died in a plane crash when Ramsay, who was ten years younger than her, was fifteen. She'd seen him through his adolescence, delaying her marriage to do so. Ramsay had spent the next few years as a part-time student of this and that, dropout, trainee at a variety of things and dole recipient.

'Somehow, he just couldn't let go of me. Phillip, my husband, eventually got sick of it. I can't blame him. Ramsay'd turn up at just the wrong times. Stay too long. Cost too much. I don't know whether Phillip and I would've made a go of it anyway, but certainly not with Ramsay hanging on. He was a sort of catalyst for our breakup.'

'Difficult,' I said, thinking: *spineless bludger.*

'This was our parents' house, where we grew up. I rented it out while I was married and moved back after the split. Phillip and I had a flat. That was sold and we divided the money. I had just enough to clear the mortgage on this place. Not enough to maintain it, really. Ramsay helped for a while, but he moved on, like always.'

So I'd read the signs wrongly. The teamwork had been between brother and sister, not husband and wife. I wasn't sure whether that was better or worse. It sounded as if Ramsay Hewitt had certain characteristics in common with Damien Talbot and that might explain their antagonism. That thought put me back on what was supposed to be my track, locating Megan French.

'Tess, you've seen Megan French and Talbot together. What's the attraction? She seems to be a pretty smart kid and he's . . .'

'I'm no psychologist. He's charming, persuasive.'

'There must be more to it than that.'

'Haven't you ever been attracted to someone who was wrong for you? I have.'

'I suppose. But not that wrong.'

'It'll be there in her background somewhere — some lack of love, abuse maybe. Some wildness. I don't know.'

'And you've no idea where Talbot could have gone?'

She shook her head but I wasn't sure that she'd taken in the question. She was off on a path of her own. 'No-one in our family's ever been arrested,' she said. 'I don't know anything about

84

bail and things like that. Do we have bail bondsmen like they do in America? You know, like in *Midnight Run*?'

'No.'

'How does it work?'

'Someone usually guarantees the amount. Puts their assets on the line.'

'Jesus. All I've got's the house. I can't lose the house.'

'You're saying Ramsay'd jump bail on you. Surely not.'

'There's no way to tell what Ramsay would do. It's not his fault, he was too young to lose his parents like that.'

I had my doubts on that score. Plenty of people took worse knocks and made out all right. And from what I'd seen Tess would have made a pretty fair substitute parent. Still, there's no knowing. I tried to tell her not worry and that the laying of the charge might be just a way to put pressure on her brother, to get him to steer the police to Talbot. And that if bail was required the amount wouldn't be too large.

'How much?'

'Tess, I don't know. Anyway, couldn't who-ever's behind the protest put up the money?'

She was suddenly alert. She put down her coffee mug and turned on me. 'What? Who?'

Wrong thing to say, Cliff, I thought, but it was too late. 'I was told that the Tadpole Creek protest has a backer of some kind. A supporter.'

'Who told you that?'

I saw where this was heading but I had no

escape route. 'Someone from the security firm.'

'What the hell are you doing talking to those Millennium bastards? God, I should have known it. You're a plant, a bloody spy. Ramsay was right.'

I tried to tell her that the Millennium people had come to me, not the other way around, and that I wasn't a spy or anything like it.

She shook her head, stood up, and her body went tight as if she was setting up a physical defence against me. 'I don't believe you. Ramsay might get a lot of things wrong, but he's got an instinct about people. He knows his enemies and he reckoned you were one.'

I was getting angry. I'd already made my judgement about Ramsay and he was right — I wasn't sympathetic, but not for the reasons he imagined. 'He's wrong this time.'

'I think you'd better go.'

11

I knew what was coming next and I was dreading it. An agitated, near-hysterical message from Cyn was on the answering machine when I reached home. She'd got the news on the radio and television and the name of one of the people the police were looking for had hit her hard. I had a shower, pulled on an old tracksuit, poured a stiff Scotch, drank half of it and called her number.

'Cyn, this is Cliff.'

'Where the hell have you been? Out screwing some low-life slut I suppose. *Go!*'

The old Cyn. The old complaint, scarcely ever justified. That 'Go' puzzled me, though.

'I've been working. What does "go" mean?'

'Not you. Never mind. Hang on.'

I heard sounds on the line — voices, a door, but couldn't make anything of it. Cyn was away for at least ten minutes and she went straight on the attack when she got back on the line. I stood it for a while and then threatened to hang up if she didn't stop.

'Don't hang up. You didn't give me all the facts,

did you? You didn't tell me this Talbot was a serious criminal no-hoper.'

'No, I didn't.'

'Why the hell not? Trying to spare me I suppose.'

'Yes.'

'Fuck you, Cliff. When someone's dying you don't have to spare them. They're facing the worst thing there is, the end of everything. When you've faced up to that, you can face up to anything else. Are you too stupid to understand that?'

I finished the drink and immediately wanted more. 'I'm sorry.'

'You're sorry. Fat lot of good that is. Where *have* you been?'

'I've been with the sister of the leader of the Tadpole Creek protest. She was there and saw some things and heard others. There's a good chance Megan wasn't . . .'

'Wasn't what? And don't try to bloody spare me.'

'Wasn't involved directly in the death and was taken against her will.'

'Okay, okay. Just a minute. I have to take a pill. Stay there.'

I nearly tore a knee ligament bolting for the bottle, the glass and the ice cube tray. I was drink in hand when she got back on the line after what seemed like a long time.

'I've still got some money, Cliff. I can hire lawyers. Oh, what about that friend of yours? Cy . . .'

'Cy's dead. He was murdered.'

'Oh, God. The life you lead.'

'We don't need to talk about lawyers yet. This isn't a Patty Hearst situation. Megan's not . . .'

'She's on the run and being named on radio and television. She must be frantic. We *have* to do something.'

I improvised. 'I'm going to look for her. Talbot's possibly left a bit of a trail. Maybe I can track him.'

'You don't sound very sure. Why aren't you doing it now then?'

'Cyn, I'm human. I'm tired. I . . .'

I was cut off by a heavy knock at the front door.

'What?'

'Sorry, there's someone at the door.'

'Thank God. Let him in, Cliff. That's all we need to say for now.'

She hung up and I sat there with my drink in one hand and the receiver in the other without the faintest idea of what was going on.

'Hello, Mr Hardy. I'm Geoffrey Samuels. It sounds a bit silly to say this, but my mother sent me.'

The porch light is dim and he was standing back a bit so it took a few beats for me to recognise him. I hope my jaw didn't drop too far. I shook the hand he held out and registered almost nothing except that he was about the same height as me.

'She said you'd recognise me from your surveillance.'

'Geoffrey. Yes. Right. Well you'd better come in.'

It was starting to make sense. Cyn had

despatched him as soon as I'd answered the phone. He'd made good time from Crows Nest, but why? He eased past me and went down the hall to the sitting room. He had a long, loose build in boots, jeans and a leather jacket. The shoulder-length hair was dark and tangled. I caught the glint of an earring. Athletic stride. I padded along after him, feeling at a decided disadvantage in bare feet, tracksuit and with a glass of whisky in my hand.

'Have a seat. What's this about, Geoffrey?'

He gave the room a neutral glance, sat and pulled out a packet of tobacco and papers. 'D'you mind?'

I shook my head and put an ashtray near him. 'Would you like a drink?'

'No thanks. I don't drink much.'

Well, I don't smoke, I thought. *So we're even.* He made the cigarette expertly and I caught the faint whiff of marijuana as he lit up.

'Does your mother know you smoke dope?'

'Yes. She tried it herself for the pain and to relax her but she didn't take to it. Pity.'

I sat down and took some whisky for the relaxing effect. 'I suppose Cyn's told you what I'm doing for her?'

He nodded. 'At first I thought it was crazy. Then she told me what you've found out and it didn't sound so crazy.'

'I haven't found out much. I still don't know whether Megan's your sister.'

'Your daughter, you mean. That is, as well.'

I shrugged.

'You don't think so?' He took a deep drag, held it and let the smoke out slowly. *Cough and you'll ruin the effect*, I thought, but he didn't.

'I just don't know. It seems possible but there could be some other explanation. The birth dates don't quite match.'

'One day.'

He was impressively on top of his brief and handling himself well. He took another drag, pinched out the butt and put it away in his pocket. I finished the drink, thought about another and decided against.

'I still don't understand what you're doing here.'

He drew a deep breath and tossed his head to get some of the long, lank hair out of his eyes. 'Mum wants me to work with you on this.'

'I don't think so.'

'She insists.'

'She can't insist.'

Suddenly, despite the good articulation, ease with dope and general self-assurance he looked very young. 'She's going to die, Mr Hardy.'

'I know.'

'I can't say no to her. I suspended from uni today as soon as she asked me to do this. She says you used to say that you could get through things quicker and better if only you had reliable help.'

'*I* said that?'

'Yeah. When you were married.'

'How long have you known about that?'

'Oh, we knew she'd been married before. So had Dad. But I guess we weren't interested in the details. It didn't seem to matter. I only found out who you were and all that today.'

I decided that I didn't want to give the kid the wrong impression, so I reached for the Scotch bottle and gave myself a refill. 'Look, if I said that, I was lying. Cyn didn't like what I did for a living and looking back I don't blame her. I wasn't around when she needed me. I would've said that just as an excuse.'

'It doesn't matter. She reckons you're going to need help with this if you're going to find ... Megan before Mum dies.'

'I don't understand. I thought ... months ...'

He shook his head and the hair flopped down, concealing his eyes, but I knew he was close to tears. 'Latest report,' he said. 'Weeks. Maybe days.'

I made coffee. He went to the toilet and the bathroom and had re-gained his composure when he returned. I spiked my coffee and invited him to relight his joint. He did. He was taking in a lot more of his surroundings now — books, tatty carpet, worn furniture, good fax and answering machine.

'You and Mum lived here?' he said after drinking some of his coffee.

'A long time ago.'

'It's a good house. Must be worth a bit.'

'It wasn't then.'

'No, I suppose not.'

'A freeway was supposed to go through it. That's how we got it cheap.'

He nodded. The idea of a freeway going

through Glebe must have seemed bizarre to him. How he felt, with his father dead and his mother on the way out, about the past I'd shared with her, was hard to judge. He finished his joint and the coffee and put the roach in his pocket. He was slumped, tired. My wallet was in the jacket hanging over the post at the foot of the stairs. I took Cyn's cheque out and waved it.

'I haven't even banked your mother's cheque.'

He sat up. 'You're not going to pull out?'

'No, I'm just making a point. I don't let clients dictate to me.'

'This is different. I can't go back to her and say you've turned me down. I think it'd kill her. This thing's all that's keeping her going.'

We looked at each other for a full minute without speaking. He was steady-eyed, determined. I could feel myself wavering. 'How do you and your sister feel about the prospect of another one, a half-sister, being sprung on you? Especially now.'

'I'm interested. Annie'd hate it.'

'Why's that?'

'She and Mum don't get along. Haven't for years. Annie'll be upset when . . . when Mum dies, but she was closer to Dad. She's got ambitions to go into business for herself. She's in advertising, like Dad was. She'll be thinking about the money. You know, Mum's estate, and how it'll be divided. I suppose if this girl does turn out to be our sister, Mum'll change her will. That's fine with me, but Annie? Shit, she'll freak. Plus she's pregnant herself. Just.'

'I see. Haven't you got enough on your plate, what with studying and your mother and that kind of trouble in the family?'

'I told you I've suspended. That's cool. I can't do anything for Mum except what she's asking me to — work with you. Annie's not my problem. At least, not yet.'

I stalled. 'What're you studying?'

'Environmental engineering.'

'What's that?'

'Like, how to plan and build things that don't fuck up the environment. So I could be useful on this Tadpole Creek thing, Mr Hardy.'

I drank some coffee and didn't say anything.

'I can drive, I'm good with computers and I can help you with that problem of yours.'

'What's that?'

'Another thing Mum said. Along the same lines. She said you always tried to be in two places at once when you worked. With me, you can. And there's something else?'

'Yes?'

'I'm about the same age as the Talbot guy. I'm more likely than you to know how he thinks than you are. I can talk to his friends and stuff like that.'

'He also sounds dangerous. How much danger have you coped with? Has your mother thought about that, I wonder?'

'I'm a rock climber. I know about danger and how to be careful.'

I was unconvinced but he had all the answers. I could play it that way for a while. 'You've sold me. Okay, we'll work together and you can report to Cyn on our progress. What's wrong?'

His lean, bony face had split into a grin. 'I've never heard anyone call Mum Cyn before. Dad called her Cynthia always. Cyn. I like it. I think I'll have a drink now if you've got some beer or wine.'

'Sure, why now?'

'Well, I won't be driving tonight, will I? I've got everything I need in the car.'

12

Geoffrey had a beer, rang his mother and left the message that I'd agreed to let him work with me, hauled a huge backpack in from his car and went to bed in the spare room. No-one had used it for a while and it was musty, but if he was going to hang around with me he'd have to learn to take the rough with the rougher.

I looked over the notes I'd written and the scraps of information I'd collected during the day. I picked up my shirt to toss it in the laundry basket and noticed a blonde hair clinging to it. The memory of Tess Hewitt came back to me sharply. I'd had strong feelings for her and I'd thought the attraction had been mutual. I stood by my bed and thought how long it was since I'd been close to a woman. The night was cold but it suddenly seemed colder. I got into bed, tracksuit and all, and turned out the light. I was tired and the Scotch had relaxed me. I got to sleep pretty quickly, but my feet were cold all night and I couldn't wake up enough to pull the extra blanket over them. All I could do was pull them up, move around, and put them where something warm had been. It doesn't work.

Geoffrey had been up for hours when I appeared about 7.30. He'd made coffee and burnt some toast. Not even the with-it young can cope with some people's toasters. He was sitting in the kitchen trying to read the headlines on the still-rolled newspaper.

'My dad hated anyone to get to the paper before him,' he said.

'I don't give a stuff,' I grunted. 'Open 'er up and do as you like.'

I poured some coffee and was pleased to see that he'd brewed it at about the right strength. 'You set the toaster on light and it toasts medium, set it on medium and it toasts dark, set it on dark and it bloody burns,' I told him.

'I'm sort of handy. I might be able to fix it.'

'I'm not. Feel free.'

He took the elastic band off the paper, unrolled it, glanced at the headlines on the front and back pages and passed it to me. 'Would you call yourself a morning person, Mr Hardy?'

'You are, obviously. I'd say I'm not exactly an early morning person. More latish morning. Okay after eight with some coffee on board. Look, we can do without the Mr Hardy stuff. Cliff'll do. I'd prefer Geoff to Geoffrey if that's all right.'

'Sure. But why?'

'Ever see *The Lion in Winter*?'

He shook his head. He'd shaved and combed his hair back but it was rebelling.

'Get the video out and have a watch. It turned me off Geoffreys.'

He grinned, unplugged the toaster and took it to the sink where he shook the crumbs out. I read the front page of the paper while I drank the coffee. The content was ninety per cent economic and ten per cent sex. With the tabloids it's the other way around. I'm not sure that either is healthy. Drugs rather than performance dominated the sports page. As a newly acquired habit, I opened up at the obituaries. An ancient bishop had died and a slightly older philosopher. Maybe they could sort it out in the hereafter. I sighed and put the paper away. Geoff wiped the toaster down and put it back on the bench.

'Semi-buggered, Cliff,' he said. 'But it'll probably last forever like that.'

I set it for medium and dropped in two slices of bread. 'Geoff, that's a bit like how I feel myself sometimes.'

He took the paper and turned to the cryptic crossword. *Jesus*, I thought, *one of those*.

He filled in a few spaces rapidly, then clicked his pen and looked at me. 'So what's our first move?'

The first move should have shattered any illusions about the romance of the private detective business Geoff might have entertained. We paid a call on Damien Talbot's mother and got precisely nowhere. According to a neighbour, the police and the media had seen the woman and then she'd packed a bag and left without saying where she was going.

It wouldn't have surprised Cyn that the second move I made with her son in tow was to call on a prostitute. I could've sent him off on some useless errand but I didn't see any point in protecting him from the harsh realities, and I had an inkling of a real use I might have for him, so it was better if he was fully in the picture.

I'd rung Annette and made the arrangement to see her strictly on a business basis — my business, not hers. She chiacked me about it, but agreed to see me. A small piece of information I'd scribbled down had assumed significance.

Annette opened the door and posed. She wore a white satin blouse with long sleeves and lots of lace on the front, a white skirt, white stockings and shoes. She had a scrap of white silk in her hair.

'My eleven o'clock gets off on his bride fantasies,' she said. 'Who's your good-looking young friend?'

We stepped into the room and I nodded to Geoff to close the door. 'This is Geoff. He's learning the ropes.'

'I could teach him a few tricks. You too, Cliff.'

'I'm sure. Knock it off, Annette. Just a few questions. I'll pay for your time.'

'Two hundred. Three if you keep the groom waiting.'

'I won't.' I gave her the money. We all sat. She rolled the notes tightly, hitched up her skirt and tucked them into the top of her stocking, making sure that we saw the suspenders and the lace panties.

'Very nice,' I said. 'Now, you told me that Talbot was impotent.'

'Right. It happens a lot. Poor things. But I don't include him in that.' She winked at Geoff who blushed furiously.

'And you gave him the name of a clinic. Which clinic?'

She adjusted the lace that came down from her wrists over the tops of her hands. She had nice, slender hands and wore a wedding ring. 'I'm not so sure I can tell you that.'

'Why not?'

'I've got a sort of arrangement with them. I get a spotter's fee you might call it. I don't think they'd like the idea of me . . .'

'Look,' I said. 'I won't mention you. No chance. You won't come into it.'

'I don't know. I've got a good deal there.'

With that sort of an arrangement it was a sure bet she'd have the name and number written down somewhere, maybe even have a card. I could find it by applying the right pressure and maybe I would have if Geoff hadn't been there.

I took out the picture of Eve French and held it in my hand. 'Annette, she's my daughter. She's on the run with this Talbot bastard and I need a lead on him. There's a chance he went to the clinic. I need the information.'

She studied me for a few very long seconds, then got up and walked out of the room. She came back and handed me a card. 'If you catch him, give him a fucking good kicking for me.'

I kissed her cheek. 'Thanks. I will. And I think you look terrific.'

'You should've seen me when I was Geoff's age.' She did a quick, expert bump and grind.

Geoff looked at me strangely as we left the building.

'You said she's your daughter. I thought you had doubts about that.'

'I do. That was just to get past her objection to telling me about the clinic.'

'Mm.'

'What does that mean?'

'Mum said you could be a bit of a shit.'

'She was right. You have to be in this game. Can you drive a manual?'

'Of course I can.'

I tossed him the keys. 'Don't get your back up. A lot of young people can't these days. How about you drive while I think.'

'Where are we going?'

We got into the car and I examined the card Annette had given me. I laughed. 'It's called Potential. "Realise your full sexual potential blah, blah." It's in Paddington. Does a North Shore type like you know his way around Paddo?'

For an answer he started the motor, dropped neatly into first and took off smoothly. He drove well, without flourishes but handling the car nicely in the traffic and maintaining a good pace. Unlike a lot of young people, he seemed to be able to do things without having music blaring at him. Maybe he was tone deaf, but I guessed he had something on his mind. I did my own think-ing and let him do his.

'She seemed like a nice woman,' he said sud-denly when we stopped at a light. 'That Annette.'

'I'd say so.'

'Umm, have you ever been with a prostitute?'

'On occasion.'

We moved off in heavy traffic and he concen-trated until he'd positioned himself where he wanted to. 'What's it like?'

I took my time in answering. Maybe I was a father, maybe I wasn't, but either way I wasn't comfortable in this kind of role. But the kid was serious and needed a response. 'Unsatisfactory, unless she happens to be a friend.'

He nodded and chewed it over. At the next stop he said, 'Got any cassettes?'

I opened the glove box and produced the only one I had. 'Edith Piaf.'

'Who?'

'French cabaret singer. Before your time.'

'I'll give it a miss. Have you been to France?'

'Yeah. A couple of times. Briefly.'

He moved out and passed a truck. 'I've never been out of Australia.'

'Plenty of time, Geoff. Plenty of time.'

'I guess. Not for Mum, though. Well, she and Dad went overseas a couple of times so I suppose she's got the memories.'

'That's about all it comes down to. What did you and your sister do when they were away?' As soon as I spoke I thought: *What am I getting into all this shit for?*

'Dad's sister, Aunt Jessie, looked after us. Out in the country. Great fun for us, we didn't mind.'

Happy families, I thought. The couple of pseudo aunts and uncles I had lived in places like Kingsford and Botany. No fun there, just more of the same. And as far as I knew no member of my family had gone overseas before I did. And my first time was to Malaya in uniform. No holiday, that.

We passed by Sydney University and Geoff gave it a brief look.

'Is that where you're studying?'

'Yep. Third year.'

'Like it?'

'Some of it. The practical stuff's okay, the theory's a bit of a drag. I don't mind taking a break for a semester.'

'How d'you get on for money?'

'Mum pays the fees and . . . shit, I forgot. I've got a part-time job in the Vet school. Cleaning up and that. I'll have to ditch it.'

'No, you won't. I'll go along with this arrangement but I won't need you twenty-four hours a day. What is it, night work?'

'Yeah, sort of. It's pretty flexible. As long as I put in the hours I can do it pretty well any time. You sure about that? I don't want to bludge off Mum any more than I do already.'

'I'm sure. Who says you're bludging?'

His driving faltered for the first time. He had to brake sharply to avoid a late lane-changer. He hit the horn angrily. 'Fuckin' Annie does.'

I remembered the conflicts I used to have with Eve over almost everything. I was beginning to like this kid. 'Take it easy,' I said. 'We want to get there in one piece.'

'Sorry, Cliff. What's going to happen next?'

I cleared my throat and unshipped my mobile. 'I'm going to pretend to be impotent and you're going to crack a computer system. Okay?'

13

The clinic was housed in one of those big Paddington terraces in a street that seemed to have speed humps every fifty metres. The house was painted white and its iron lace was black. The fence was in good repair and the narrow front garden was neat. The contrast with my place in Glebe couldn't have been more marked. A discreet brass plaque by the gate indicated professional activities went on here but was vague about the details. I'd told Geoff how I hoped things would go and what he was to do if they did.

'That's illegal,' he said.

'So's kidnapping.'

'We don't know that's happened or anything like it.'

'Well, let's try and find out what *has* happened.'

We mounted the steps to the porch and I pressed the buzzer. The door opened and we went into the standard hallway that had been blocked off before the stairs. The block steered you into the front room where there were chairs, a table with magazines and a receptionist behind a desk. She wore a version of a nurse's uniform and was middle-aged and comfortable looking.

'Can I help you?'

'My name's Hardy. I rang a little while ago for an appointment.'

'Ah, yes, Mr Hardy. And this is . . .?'

'Geoff. My son. He's here to lend me moral support. I'm a bit anxious about this.'

'How nice,' she said. 'There's certainly no need to be anxious. If Geoff can just wait here. I'll get some details from you. I take it you're in a health fund.'

I said I was and gave her the details.

'Fine. I'll take you through to the patients' waiting room and see how long until Dr Pradesh can see you.'

I nodded to Geoff and let her lead me away, moving as slowly as I could. We went through a passage that had been created by partitions to a small room at the back of the house, one of three. There had been a lot of dividing of space back here.

'Please wait here, Mr Hardy. I'll have to ask you not to leave the room until you are called for.'

'Why's that?'

'Our patients demand and expect privacy. I'm sure you understand.'

'Of course.' I tried to look as if I'd be worried that someone would see me there. Come to think of it, if I was impotent, I would be.

I delayed her for as long as I could with a few questions but she was obviously keen to get back to her station. The magazines were soft-core pornography and there was a stack of videos of

106

the same kind on a shelf. Good healthy in-out, in-out stuff. I leafed through, admiring the supple bodies and feeling distinct stirrings. I had an image of Annette doing it in her bride's outfit with a man in a dinner jacket. I was smiling when the doctor opened the door.

'Mr Hardy? Would you come this way, please.'

He was Indian or Pakistani; small, neat, with a winning smile. We went into his surgery and assumed the traditional postures — him behind his desk, me in front. Doctor and patient, god and non-god.

'You are having trouble with your erections? Is that achieving or sustaining?'

'Both.'

'I see.' He made a note. 'Otherwise you are in good health? You look fit.'

'Fit enough,' I said. 'I've got a touch of sugar. Controlled by diet.'

Another note. 'Heart? Kidneys?'

'Recently checked and okay.'

'Do you smoke?'

I shook my head.

'Drink?'

'Moderately,' I said, giving myself a fair bit of latitude.

He took down the details of my age, medical history and occupation which I gave as 'security officer'. I gave him the name of my doctor, Ian Sangster, who'd confirm any lie I told. I claimed to have a partner who was aware of the steps I was taking.

He gave me a fairly thorough examination,

paying particular attention to my eyes. Then he reached into his desk for a pair of surgical gloves. 'Please remove your jacket and lower your trousers and underwear so that I may make an examination.'

I did and he did. He examined my genitals and probed my prostate. I stood and tried to think that at least I was getting paid for it.

'Thank you. Please sit on the examination table.'

He stripped off the gloves and dumped them in a bin. Then he put on another pair and began fiddling with a bottle, a syringe and a plastic device.

I was alarmed. 'What the hell is that for? Excuse me, doctor, but I thought . . . Viagra.'

'Indicated in some cases, not in yours. One of the side-effects of Viagra is interference with the eyesight. Unimportant mostly, but with that old damage to your eye, not to be risked.'

'I see.'

'You should not worry. The therapy simply involves injecting the penis with a combination of substances including prostoglandin. These permit the blood to flow past any blockages or narrownesses and facilitate an erection. The device is spring-loaded and enables you to do the injection without discomfort or pain. What I am going to do now is give you a tiny dose to check your reaction. Both my examination and your medical history suggest that you are a suitable subject for this therapy. Do you wish to proceed?'

Reluctant wasn't the word, but I nodded. He

showed me how to use the injection kit. A click, a slight sting and it was done.

'I will now ask Mrs Merryweather to prepare the waiting room where you can watch a video for a few moments. Then I can check the results.'

'Okay,' I said. I was thinking: *Fine, more time for Geoff to do his stuff.*

He spoke to Mrs M and it was quite a few minutes before she buzzed him back. He showed me into the waiting room again and I settled down to watch a bearded man fuck a woman who had hair only on her head. He did it well in several positions. He appeared to enjoy it more than she did but he might just have been a better actor. It was pretty undemanding in that sense. Dialogue was minimal. Glen Withers and I used to watch porn from time to time for fun and this was fair average quality stuff. I usually responded but not as quickly or as strongly as this. I found myself getting uncomfortably hard.

Dr Pradesh returned and we went back into his surgery. Down came the strides and underpants and on went the rubber gloves. I was fully erect and he stood and looked at me.

'That's impressive, Mr Hardy.'

'I'm very encouraged, Doctor.'

'I imagine so. Well, I usually give patients a six month supply of the medication, but in your case I suspect your problem is basically psychological and I would be hopeful that a few successful episodes of intercourse would help considerably. Ah, you may adjust your clothing.'

'Thanks, doctor,' I said as I struggled to stuff

myself back inside my pants, and they were by no means tight. 'I'd say I feel better already.'

He smiled. 'If you will wait a few minutes out at reception Mrs Merryweather will supply you. I'll just check that the coast is clear.'

He established that and we shook hands.

'Hurry home, Mr Hardy.'

'I will, doctor. I will.'

Geoff gave me a nod as I re-joined him in the waiting room. Mrs Merryweather looked anxiously at her watch and I guessed that another patient was due to come out into public view. She got the buzz from inside, whipped away and returned with a cardboard container about half the size of a shoe box.

'Your medication, Mr Hardy. Plus syringes, swabs and the injection device. With the consultation fee that comes to two hundred and eighty dollars. Part of the cost of the medication is reclaimable from your health fund.'

I wrote a cheque and took the box. She gave me a receipt and a motherly smile. I thanked her. 'It seems to be a marvellous treatment.'

She said, 'Oh, yes, oh, yes,' and I'd have bet a thousand bucks that she and Mr Merryweather were satisfied customers.

We got outside and I drew in a deep breath. Geoff jiggled the car keys. 'Want to drive?'

'No. How'd you go?'

'I think I can do it. I'll have to get my laptop. Might have to talk to someone who's cluey on this sort of thing.'

'I thought *you* were cluey.'

110

'Can always use help. Why're you so shitty? Weird place, that. You can hear people moving around but you don't see anyone. What did they do to you in there?'

'Never mind. I need a drink. Several drinks.'

'Why're you walking funny?'

'Am I?'

'Yes, you are.'

'Son, I've got a hard-on that Gary Cooper would've been proud of.'

'Who's Gary Cooper?'

'Just drive.'

14

Thirty years ago, Sydney University students lived in Glebe and Newtown in ratty terraces and crumbling squats. Gentrification forced them slowly west, to Annandale and Leichhardt and then further out towards Marrickville and even beyond. Geoffrey Samuels shared a house with three other students in Lewisham. It wasn't a bad looking house but it was easy to see why it was a better proposition as a student rental than owner-occupied — there was a main road out front, a factory next door and the train line ran right past the back fence.

Being a polite young man, Geoffrey invited me in, but I'd seen all the student houses I ever wanted to see and opted to stay outside, saying I had phone calls to make. For a minute I thought he was going to ask me who to, which would have been difficult to answer because I was lying. In fact I wanted to get out of the car and stand somehow so that I didn't feel I had a salami inside my pants. Maybe a few deep breaths of fresh air would help.

Geoff shrugged and bowled up to the house

with his hair flying in the breeze, a quick spring taking him to the top of the front steps in one jump. That action reminded me of the Tadpole Creek protest and Tess's account of Megan French as a springheel Jack. The thought sobered me after the farce of the clinic and I tried to focus back on what we were doing. I had no real reason to suspect that Talbot would harm Megan seriously, but he sounded unstable to start with and the pressure he must be under now wouldn't help.

Geoff disappeared inside and after a few minutes a young woman came out, leaned in the open doorway and looked at me. She was large and overweight and if she stayed where she was Geoff would have trouble getting past her. Maybe that was her plan. I wondered what he'd told her about me that had excited her interest. I tried to look nonchalant as I mimed making a phone call. She looked disgusted and vanished.

Anti mobile phones, I thought. That's okay, so am I.

Geoff came back carrying something not very heavy in a not very big case. He deposited it on the back seat carefully and got behind the wheel.

'What did you tell your housemate about me?' I asked. 'She came out to get an eyeful.'

'Oh, Jules. Yeah. I told her you were my uncle.'

'Well, I am one. I'm an anti-godfather, too.'

He started the car and I was pleased to see that he didn't rev it unnecessarily. 'What's that?'

'A godfather who doesn't believe in God. How long's this going to take?'

'All depends.'

113

Ask an ignorant question, get a non-informative answer.

Back at my place I left him in the spare room plugged in to the phone line I had installed upstairs when I'd toyed with the idea of getting on the e-mail and Internet myself. So far, I hadn't done anything about it, but the day was coming. Down below I phoned Cyn, got her machine, and told her that Geoff and I were getting along okay but there were no further developments. It's easier to lie to a machine than face-to-face with a person dying of cancer.

I itched to know how the police were doing in their hunt for Talbot, but since Glen Withers left me and Frank Parker retired, I've lost my access to information the police don't necessarily want citizens to know about. It was time for me to set about cultivating another contact but it's got harder to do. Friendship was always the best method and money came next. These days, both avenues have more or less closed down except in peripheral areas like motor registration and such because cops have become paranoid and suspicious. Understandably. The funny thing is that the 'cop culture' all the reformers wanted to crack open has just hardened under the pressure.

It's much the same with the journalists. Back when they worked for owners, not corporations, and could smoke and drink in the office, they were willing to tell you things off the record in exchange for off-the-record information from you. Not any more; now the news is so processed and sanitised almost nothing gets out that could ruffle corporate feathers. The politicians take some heat occasionally, but the money men are safe. A journalist these days would rather find out that Princess Diana had had an ingrowing toenail than that the head of a multinational had embezzled a hundred million.

Well, with my computer expert working upstairs at least I was moving with the times. I took him a cup of coffee and inhaled a little of the marijuana smoke.

'How's it going?'

'Getting there. The security's not as good as it should be. She left the server software in a desk drawer, so that was easy. Now I have to get the user to get into the data base.'

'How will you do that?'

'It'll be something they can all remember — the name of the receptionist or one of the doctors, the street they're in — something like that. I collected a up a few cards while I was there.'

'You're a natural.'

He took a sip of his coffee and a drag on his joint. 'Leave me with it, unless you can help.'

'Just be as quick as you can. I've got another job for you when you finish that.'

'Okay. What's my rate of pay?'

'Room and board, son, room and board. D'you know the paperwork involved in actually employing someone these days?'

'Yeah, the country's fucked.'

'Not quite. But they're trying.'

I left him to it and discovered, when I got downstairs, that my erection had subsided. It was the first time I'd ever been relieved about that. Out of curiosity I opened the box Mrs Merryweather had given me and removed several packets of fine needles designated for injecting insulin; the plastic injection kit and a leaflet on how to use it, another leaflet on priapism (a possible and very unwelcome side effect of the treatment), and a small bottle of the magic elixir. I studied the leaflets. 'STORE IN REFRIGERATOR' the sticker on the bottle read, so I did.

'Hey, Cliff!'

I raced up the stairs, glad to have that freedom of movement back.

'Got it?'

'Yep. I'm in and they haven't password-protected the files.' Geoff pointed to the screen where Damien Talbot's file was set out in large type. The doctor had been more thorough with him than Dr Pradesh had been with me. Talbot's height and weight were recorded along with his pulse rate and blood pressure. He had described himself as a social drinker and admitted to smoking twenty cigarettes a day. The injury to his foot ('damage to ligaments in ankle and foot') was noted. Talbot had claimed to be in a permanent relationship and to have been impotent for the past year.

The doctor's notes indicated his scepticism: 'Patient's fingers heavily nicotine-stained; evidence of drug injection; blood pressure high, pulse fast, lung capacity poor.' No medication had been prescribed pending a report from Talbot's own doctor. The final note wasn't comforting:

'Patient violent and abusive'. I copied down the address Talbot had given and the name and address of his doctor, Dr Bruce Macleod.

'Good work, Geoff. The address's likely to be phoney but the doctor's probably genuine.'

'How do you figure that? And why's the doctor so important?'

'I've been told Talbot lives mainly in the van and anyone dodging fines the way he's been doing wouldn't give out his address easily. But my guess is he wanted the impotence treatment badly enough to stick to the track where he could. At least up until it looked as if he wasn't going to get his way.'

'Okay.'

'The doctor's the only bit of hard information we've got on him, and he's got plenty of health problems — a crook leg, a broken thumb, drugs, sex. There's a chance the doctor'll be able to tell me what he might do next, how dangerous he is. Stuff like that.'

'I get it. *If* he'll talk to you.'

'There's that.'

Geoff made a series of moves with the mouse. The slimline printer kicked on and he handed me a printout of the file. I expected a cheeky remark but he wasn't looking amused. 'Sounds like a real shit, this bloke.'

I shrugged. 'He's said to be charming when he wants to be.'

He turned the computer off and pushed his chair back. 'So, do we go and see the doctor?'

'I do, you don't. Doctors can be difficult.

They're litigious and I've already violated the conditions of my licence by getting you to do what you've done. If I show up with you in tow . . .'

'Well, we're in the same boat. It's illegal to hack into medical records.'

'All the more reason for you to stay out of it. No, I've got something else for you to do. Something you can do better than me.'

'You don't often hear people your age saying that. What is it?'

'I want you to go to Tadpole Creek and see if you can get yourself in somehow. As you pointed out yourself, you're an environmental engineer. You must know the lingo. You could be doing a thesis or something. You'll have to watch yourself. They're not dumb. Particularly a woman named Tess Hewitt. She's the sister of one of the leaders of the protest, Ramsay.'

'Okay. What am I trying to find out?'

'This Ramsay Hewitt got himself arrested in connection with the death of the security guard. I'd like to know how that stands. But the most important thing is to find out who's backing the protest. Putting up the money and supplying equipment and so on.'

'I thought the most important thing was to find Talbot.'

'It is, but I've got a feeling there's a connection. There's something not quite right about this protest.'

'Like what?'

'I don't know. I'll show you the stuff I've got on the history of the site and you can make up your own mind. Are you all right to drive after smoking dope?'

'One joint? Sure.'

'Watch yourself with that when you're out there. I'm not sure of their attitude to it.'

He stood up and stretched and his fingers almost reached the ceiling. 'How long've they been there?'

'A couple of months I think.'

He laughed. 'They're probably growing it.'

We went downstairs and like a well brought up young person he took his coffee mug with him and rinsed it. I gave him the stuff I'd taken off the Net about Homebush and the material Smith had left. He wasn't impressed. 'I'm sure I could come up with more than this.'

'Later. Here's a key to the house and the number here and at the office and of the mobile. You can leave messages on all three so stay in touch.'

'You're sure you're not fobbing me off with some bullshit job while you do the real work?'

'No. And keep an eye out for Megan French.'

'How'll I know her?'

'She's tall and dark, bit beaky-nosed and she can do a four-metre long-jump in hiking boots.'

'Your daughter in other words.'

'Your sister, maybe. And don't mention me, of course.'

15

I located Dr Macleod's number in the phone book, rang him and got a male secretary. I stated my business in very general terms and secured an appointment to see the good doctor at 3 pm. That gave me some time to fill in so I took my Smith & Wesson .38 apart and cleaned and oiled it. I hadn't fired it in a long time and wasn't anxious to again, but Talbot, a drug-user and violence-prone, sounded dangerous and I had a feeling I was getting closer to him. The .38's not a heavy gun, and it sat snugly in a lightweight holster under my left armpit, easily concealed by any kind of loose fitting jacket. I've found though, that I tend to move differently when wearing a gun, stand, sit and walk differently, so I strapped it on and kept it there to get used to the feeling while I ate a sandwich and a couple of bananas and drank a cup of caffeinated coffee.

It didn't surprise me to find my friend and medical adviser, Dr Ian Sangster, smoking and drinking black coffee in his break from surgery at 1 pm. What did surprise me was that he was smoking a filter cigarette and the coffee packet beside his percolator had the word 'decaffeinated' printed on it. Sangster was noted for his complete refusal to follow what he called 'medical correctness'. He ate fast food, smoked, drank a lot, imbibed a dozen cups of coffee every day and didn't exercise. He looked permanently exhausted but had boundless energy. I tapped the packet.

'What's this, Ian? My faith in you is in danger of shattering.'

He took a deep drag on the cigarette and butted it. 'Don't worry. It's only for six months. I'm giving medical correctness a trial. I'll go in for tests and see if there's any bloody difference in anything. You'd have been more astonished if you'd seen me at six this morning.'

'How's that?'

'Walking. For half an hour.'

'Mm. I think medical correctness'd advise cutting out the fags altogether. What about the grog?'

'White wine only.'

'How much?'

'Stuff you. To what do I owe the pleasure?' He lit another filter and made a face as he tasted the smoke. 'I've got a clinic in half an hour, less if they're scratching at the door.'

This would be the free-as-air session Ian lays on for the indigent of Glebe, of whom, despite the rents, rates and mortgages, there are still quite a few tucked away here and there. I poured myself a cup of coffee and tasted it. It wasn't bad and it reminded me that I hadn't said anything about food to Geoff. No doubt he'd make his own arrangements.

'I'm interested in a colleague of yours, Ian. Dr Bruce Macleod. In Flemington. Know anything about him?'

One of Ian's activities, along with drinking, smoking and eating like Elvis Presley, is his membership of innumerable medical bodies — discussion groups, tribunals, policy framing committees. Network should be his middle name. He shook his head and sucked in more smoke which came out in little gusts as he spoke. 'Doesn't ring any bells. Can you leave it with me?'

'Not for long. I've got an appointment with him in a couple of hours.'

'I'll make some calls and get you on your mobile if anything turns up.'

I strolled back home wondering if Geoff had left yet. When I'd gone off to see Ian he'd been still at the computer fiddling with something I didn't bother asking about, figuring I wouldn't understand it anyway. I caught him as he was getting into his car.

'Just going,' he said.

'Need petrol money or anything like that?'

He shook his head and drove off.

To Melburnians Flemington signifies racehorses, to Sydneysiders it means a fruit and vegetable market. It's about the only example I can think of where Melbourne sounds more exciting than

Sydney. I was struck by the proximity of Flemington to Homebush, the basic area of operations in this case. What had I told Geoff? That I had a feeling there was a connection of some kind at work here. But experience has taught me not to trust intuition any more than halfway. This could be sheer coincidence.

I was early and I sat in the car waiting for a call from Ian. It came, breaking in on a fantasy I was having about what might follow if Megan French was my daughter. I saw us on Maroubra beach where I'd spent nine-tenths of my time when I was young.

'Ian?'

'You're anxious and I have to be quick. How this bloke's kept his licence to practise is a tribute to the incompetence of the legal system. Talk about negligence suits. Someone should write to Evan Whitton about it.'

'Dodgy?'

'Decidedly. A slave to the health funds, a collaborator with plastic surgeons, a pill pusher, a quack for hire. Doesn't do much hands-on doctoring and what he does he botches. What's he up to now?'

'I'm after a low-life who's got a problem with a crippled leg, impotence and at a guess psychotic tendencies. Plus a history of drug use and violence.'

'Just exactly Macleod's sort of patient. He's probably supplying him with heroin and helping him with his worker's compensation or welfare fiddle in return for a cut.'

123

'So he's unlikely to supply me with information about one of his patients?'

'Not at all. It'd depend on how much you were willing to pay him.'

'And what sort of a bloke is Macleod himself? Tough?'

'No. Obese, I'm told. A butterball. But he's got some nasty types on the payroll, according to my source. Watch yourself, Cliff. You can only break certain bones in the human body so many times.'

It was my day for visiting clinics. Dr Macleod's set-up went under the name of the Macleod Medical Clinic, according to the brass plate on the gate that gave pedestrian access. This was beside a drive-way, also gated, and set into a high brick fence surrounding a half-acre block that commanded a good view across to the vast sprawl of Rookwood cemetery. The brass plate also listed Dr Macleod's various degrees and diplomas. It was hard to guess from some of the initials exactly what medical fields they covered — and the institutions that had awarded them weren't mentioned.

For me, I was dressed formally. Not the suit, but I'd exchanged my usual casual jacket for a blazer, my jeans for a pair of charcoal slacks and I had on a clean blue button-down shirt and black slip-ons. No tie. I fancied I looked the part of an energetic semi-professional pursuing his lawful occupation. The gun under my arm was licensed after all, even if the one held on a clip under the dashboard of the Falcon wasn't and the lock picks attached to my key ring would cause any alert policeman to take them from me, put me behind some bars and see how I got on from there.

The wall was two metres high with a strand or two of razor wire on top. Top security. Maybe the doctor collected Old Masters. I pressed the intercom buzzer beside the gate, got a recorded message and stated my business. There was a humming noise and the gate clicked open. Inside I noted grass and cement in about equal amounts; a well-tended native garden with seats and benches. It looked as if the doc liked his patients to sit in the sunshine while they waited for him — or while they wrote out their cheques afterwards. I realised that I was making judgements on the basis of Ian Sangster's information. Why not?

The main building was a long, low piece of colonial architecture, much modified over about a hundred years. A series of signs directed deliveries to the back, patients to one verandah entrance, business callers to another. My visit to the other clinic had filled me with confidence about my robust health; I was here on business.

I responded to a 'Please Open' sign on a door and found myself in a waiting room that resembled something you'd see in an accountant's office. Leather armchairs, low table, business magazines. A disembodied voice said, 'Please make yourself comfortable. Dr Macleod will be with you in a moment. Please avail yourself of the refreshment facilities.' This meant a coffee machine and a fresh juice dispenser. I made a cup of coffee and sat down. The seat hissed under me the way well-upholstered vinyl pretending to be leather will and I felt better. The coffee was lousy.

A second door opened and a huge man entered the room. He was over 190 centimetres and built like Sydney Greenstreet; chalk him down for 140 kilos. I began to get up but he moved quickly and had to bend down slightly to offer me his hand.

'Mr Hardy,' he said in a strong Scots accent, rolling the Rs. 'I'm Bruce Macleod.'

The hand was soft from the heel pad to the fingertips. Shaking hands with him was like mixing dough.

'Afternoon, doctor. Good of you to see me.'

He wore a double-breasted business suit, grey with a muted pinstripe, a white shirt and burgundy silk tie. His appearance said, 'I'm wealthy and successful.' I wondered what sort of patients responded to that. He bent at the knees to support his weight and lowered himself into a chair.

'Not a medical matter, I believe.'

'It is and it isn't. I'm a private detective as I told your . . .'

'Secretary. Yes.'

'Right and I'm looking for information about one of your patients.'

'Damien Talbot. Most unfortunate. I've heard of the trouble he's in.'

'It seems he's seldom been out of trouble. I'm working for the mother of the young woman who's with him. Naturally, she's concerned about her daughter. I want to find Talbot and get the girl away from him.'

'Anticipating the police, I take it?'

He was probing. It suggested that the police

hadn't yet made the connection to him. A marginal advantage to me, possibly. 'That wouldn't hurt.'

'I see. And what d'you want from me, Mr Hardy?'

He was a smooth number, self-assured, confident — almost arrogant. Not a guy to threaten, maybe a guy to flatter. 'First,' I said, 'your professional assessment of Talbot. How dangerous is he? How serious is his physical impairment? Anything you can tell me along those lines. I know there'll be limitations to what you can reveal.'

He frowned and tented his fat fingers. 'Very severe limitations I'm afraid. And secondly?'

'Can you help me to find him?'

'Help how?'

'Can you get in touch with him?'

He smiled, revealing expertly capped teeth. It struck me that he was vain, despite his bulk. In fact he gave the impression of being proud of every kilo and their arrangement. 'Help you to trap him in other words.'

'I wouldn't put it quite like that.'

'I daresay you wouldn't. I'm afraid I'll have to think this over, Mr Hardy.'

'Why's that?'

He frowned. 'As you suggested, there's a serious matter of confidentiality involved.'

'There's also the public interest.'

'And your own.'

'You're being offensive.'

I recognised the technique. This guy was a master at putting you on the defensive. I struggled to get back into the action, considered mentioning the police, but he didn't give me the chance. He was levering himself up and he was just a touch short of breath when he gained his feet. 'As I say, Mr Hardy. I'll consider what you've put to me. It's not something to be undertaken lightly. I take it my secretary can get in touch with you?'

He glided out on what I suddenly realised were very small feet. Twinkle toes. I stayed where I was and waited for the announcement. It came a few seconds later. 'Please leave the waiting room.' I sat still and looked around. The camera could've been anywhere but I made guess at the ventilator high in the wall opposite me. From there a swivel mounted camera could survey the whole room. I poured the cold coffee into a vase of flowers, put up two fingers and left the room.

Once outside the building I expected to be escorted to the gate but no-one appeared so I drifted around to the back to see what else the doctor had on the premises. A four-berth carport with two 4WDs at home, several small Besser-block buildings and another drive-in entrance. Back here grass gave way altogether to concrete and the whole area gave off an air of high secu-rity. As I stood there in the weak sunshine with the breeze cutting into me, a man emerged from the main building. He was stocky and looked uncomfortable in his suit as if his natural uniform was more like mine — something allowing quick movement and travel over rough ground.

'Help you, sir?'

From the nicely balanced way he stood, he looked more ready to hit than help.

'Not really. I've just seen the doctor . . .'

'And now you're leaving. The gate's that way.'

He pointed but not the way an untrained person points, not so as to disturb that precise balance. He was about my size but a good deal younger and I didn't fancy a physical contest with him even if there'd been something to gain from it. I wondered if I could get the edge in other ways.

'Right,' I said. 'Just off. What goes on there?' I pointed to one of the small buildings and let my jacket come open so he could see the .38. He did, but it didn't faze him.

'That's the doctor's library. The other building is a pathology laboratory.'

'Uh huh. Well, I'm on my way.'

He said nothing but I could feel his eyes on my spine as I walked away, around the main building towards the front. A button released the gate and I went out to where the air was free to breathe and there was no-one watching your every move. Or so I thought.

I was irritated and dissatisfied. I had questions: how often did Talbot see the doctor; when did he last see him; what was the nature of their relationship? Macleod wasn't going to tell me and neither was the well-balanced attendant. I looked along the street. The clinic occupied at least two frontages with a vacant block on one side and a paved car park serving a small electronics factory on the other. Privacy. Opposite, it was a different story. The houses on large blocks had deep gardens. Some were double-storeyed behind high hedges; some were set close to the street and some further back. I wondered if there were any sticky-beaks, nosey-parkers, snoops behind those hedges and gates. You never know.

I decided to try my luck at the houses and started at the end of the street, a hundred metres or so from the clinic. I took a risk, saying that I was from the sheriff's office with a warrant to serve. The ID card I carried to that effect was legitimate but specific to the warrant it related to and long out of date, but it opened some doors. I asked several women, one man and an adolescent with a heavy cold if they'd ever seen Talbot's van and learned nothing. At a house almost opposite the clinic, the door was opened by a small, elderly woman of the kind that used to be called a little old lady.

Standing on the doorstep she barely reached to my chest which made her not much over five feet in the old measure. She had white hair but her blue eyes still had a lot of colour and were bright. Her hands were well worn and the skin on her face was finely lined rather than wrinkled. She held her thin body very straight. I guessed her age at about eighty but judged there was still plenty of mileage left in her.

The path up to the house was flanked by lines of tall pines and other trees dominated in the garden and the temperature was several degrees lower than out in the street — nice in summer, a bit chilly for now. The woman was dressed for it in slacks and a heavy cable-knit sweater. I gave her my spiel and she looked at me as if she was considering calling the dog. *Another miss*, I thought, and put the card away.

'I'm sorry to bother you,' I said.

'It's all right, I'm not bothered. I'm thinking.'

More promising. I stayed put.

'You're not a policeman, are you?'

'No.'

She pointed at the clinic. 'If you're working for that man I'll say good day to you, but I have a feeling you're not.'

'I'm sorry. I don't know what you have in mind but . . .'

'You're not working for that man?'

She really had my interest now. It's rare for people to deny doctors their title and it generally means something when they do. I more or less followed suit by stating that I wasn't working for Macleod.

'I thought not when I saw you in there. I can tell you things about him if you're interested.'

Batty, I thought, *but possibly useful*. 'You saw me in there?'

'I can see into the place from my second-floor window.' She touched the spectacles she wore. 'I can see very well with these. I saw you with one of his thugs and I could tell that you weren't getting on from the way you both moved.'

'Could you? And why are you so interested in what goes on over there?' I thought it was time to produce the card again. 'You are?'

131

'Miss Mirabelle Cartwright. I've seen that van you asked about, too.'

Bingo. 'Perhaps we could talk inside.'

'Yes, you see, that man murdered my sister.'

16

I stared at her.

'You think I'm mad, don't you?'

'Not at all.'

Her look was shrewd. 'You're not what you say you are, I believe. Your behaviour over there was quite odd. I must say you put that card you showed me away very quickly and it looked rather old. Would you care to show it to me again? I'd like to check the date on it.'

I was looking for a watcher and I'd found one, mad or not. I admitted that I wasn't serving warrants and showed her my credentials.

'Let's talk,' she said.

Two minutes later I was inside her house and the jug was on for tea. There are certain very rare circumstances when I'll drink tea and this was one of them. Miss Cartwright's house was an old weatherboard, something like a Queenslander, except much narrower and with a high loft room in the front. She took me up the steep staircase and showed me how the window of the loft afforded a view between the trees into the Macleod compound. I hadn't doubted her but she seemed to want to establish her bona fides.

Her house was well-kept but not fussy. Surfaces were clean rather than polished, and in the kitchen where we were going to drink the tea, gardening gloves, books and a pair of Wellington boots lay around where they could be got at rather than where they could've been more tidily placed. She took off her glasses and put them on a table. 'I don't need them inside and I've got other ones for reading.'

I nodded. I didn't need any more convincing that her vision was okay. A grey tabby wandered through and went on its way without comment from its owner. At least Miss Cartwright wasn't a dotty or obsessive cat fancier. So far, so good.

Mirabelle Cartwright told me that she and her sister, Beatrix, had lived all their lives in this house which had belonged to their parents. Neither had married and both had retired from jobs in the public service on small but adequate pensions. Beatrix had gone to Macleod for treatment for her arthritis and had, according to her sister, 'fallen under his evil spell'.

'That man seduced her. I don't mean in the nasty sense. I mean that he took her over, body and soul. She altered her will without my knowledge and left her half of the house to him and not to me, breaking our agreement of thirty years' standing.

'He prescribed steam baths and ice baths and I don't know what else for the poor soul. She was dead within a year of first seeing him. At first I thought it was just, you know, fate. Beatrix had never been as healthy as me. I would've expected her to live well beyond seventy-three all the same. Our parents both lived into their nineties and our brothers . . .' She broke off.

I sipped my tea and didn't say anything.

'They were fine young men, athletes. They could swim like fish and run like the wind. They were both killed in the war. Both.'

I was becoming more sceptical by the minute. The Cartwrights seemed to have run into more than their share of bad luck. Australian casualties in World War II weren't that high. For two brothers to be killed must have been a rarity, whereas in the Great War it was commonplace. And doctors have a peculiar appeal for some single women. The scepticism must have shown on my face because she put down her cup sharply so that it rattled in the saucer. 'You don't believe me.'

'I don't know.'

'You think that because I live here under that man's sufferance . . . Oh, yes he could compel me to sell up at any time . . . my mind is poisoned against him.'

She was a very acute person, something like that was *exactly* what I'd been thinking.

'Well, you're wrong, Mr Hardy. I'm not the only one, you see. I asked around down at the elderly citizens' club and much the same thing had happened to several other people. They'd lost people after that man had started treating them and for some of them it was worse.'

She really had me now. 'In what way, Miss Cartwright?'

She leaned forward and hissed the words. 'They *disappeared.*'

I was doubtful again. I needed something stronger than tea to cope with all this. I sat back in my chair and gave her a hard look. 'You notified the police of course.'

She shook her neat head. Her still thick, silvery hair fell forward and she brushed it back impatiently. It occurred to me that she would have been attractive when young and she still had vitality. I wondered what had caused her life to run on the track it had. In a very short space of time I'd heard about long-living parents, athletic brothers and a sick sister. Who was it said that a dysfunctional family is any with more than one member?

'No, I didn't go to the police about Beatrix,' she said. 'What could I prove? I thought about going when those people told me about the disappearances but I thought too long. Two were quite old and they died not that long after I spoke with them. That left only Mrs Barnes and I have to admit that she's not quite all there any more.'

'I see.'

She looked at her wristwatch. 'I generally have a whisky about now. Would you care for one, Mr Hardy?'

Recipe for a long life, I thought, and said that I'd like a whisky. She had a decanter on a tray on a drinks trolley along with some glasses. She went to the kitchen and came back with a soda siphon and a bowl of ice. Working on the top of the trolley, she dropped one cube into a glass, poured a single finger and filled the glass with soda. She

136

pushed the makings towards me. 'Make yourself a decent one,' she said. 'My father used to say that drowning good whisky was a crime. Mind you, he was talking about Scotch and this is Irish whisky. I haven't been able to abide Scots things since . . .'

I made a solid drink and took a good slug of it. I rolled the liquor around in my mouth and let it slide down. Whatever the top of the line Irish whisky might be, this was it. In the old days I would've rolled a cigarette, had another drink and hoped for the chemical stimulus to produce an insight. Now, the alcohol had to do it alone. Sometimes it felt like flying with one wing.

'Miss Cartwright,' I said. 'I'm still not sure why you've told me all this.'

She pecked at her drink like a hummingbird. 'But you're interested?'

'Yes.'

'I thought you would be. When I saw a resourceful-looking person go in and come out so quickly I guessed that you and that man hadn't seen eye to eye. And when I saw what happened between you and the thug I felt convinced of it.'

'I think he has some involvement with the man I'm looking for. But it's just a suspicion. You have to be very careful with doctors, they . . .'

'I'm sure he has a lot of things to hide. Who is this person?'

'Do you watch the news on television or listen to the radio news?'

'Sometimes, not lately.'

I told her about the death of the guard at Tadpole Creek and my interest in the matter

137

without mentioning any names. I mentioned Talbot's van again.

'I've certainly seen that van over there. It goes in through that back entrance.'

'How often have you seen it?'

She tapped her fingers on the table. 'Oh, my memory for something like that is so bad. More than once or twice is all I could be sure of.'

I thought back quickly. There'd been two vehicles in the carport. Neither was a van. 'Have you seen it recently?'

She sipped her pale drink. 'I really couldn't say. Of course I don't keep a watch on the place all the time. I've got a garden to attend to and shopping to do and so on.'

I finished the drink and stood up. 'This has all been very interesting, Miss Cartwright and I think you've been of some help. If Macleod's involved in the matter I'm looking into I'll try to see that he gets into serious trouble. You can get me on these numbers pretty well any time. Let me know if you see the van or the young man who drives it. The one with the limp.'

She took the card that I held out. 'And the young woman I've seen. Who is she exactly?'

'I wish I knew.'

She shook her head. 'I think you do know.'

'She may be my daughter.'

Her nod was wise, compassionate, concerned — all that.

17

I was sitting in the car wondering what to do next when my mobile bleated.

'Hardy.'

'This is Tess Hewitt, Cliff. I'm sorry about what happened the other night. I over-reacted.'

'It's okay, Tess. I'm glad you called. I didn't mean to upset you but this bloody business I'm in requires it sometimes. Anyway, what's new?'

'Well, you were right. Bill Damelian didn't have any trouble getting bail for Ramsay and he doesn't think the charge'll proceed. So I should've listened to you.'

'That's good. Where's Ramsay now? I'd like to talk to him.'

'God, you do stick at it, don't you? He's doing something for one of the television stations about the protest. He said he feels terrible about the guard but . . .'

'The publicity's good.'

'He's young, Cliff. I sort of hoped you might want to talk to *me*.'

She hadn't really answered the question about Ramsay's whereabouts and I wanted to put the same question I'd put to her, to him: who was the Tadpole Creek protest's benefactor? She misinterpreted my pause.

'All right, then. You don't want to see me again. I . . .'

'Tess, Tess, don't get me wrong. I do want to see you. Right now. Where are you?'

I was hoping she wasn't at the protest. The last thing I wanted to do was crowd Geoff.

'I'm at home,' she said. 'Please come, and you can ask me anything you want. I promise I won't fly off the handle.'

There's nothing like resolving a conflict to bring people closer. Tess said hello and touched my arm. I walked into the house with a companionable feeling that was rapidly becoming something more than that. We had a drink and more or less repeated our phone conversation. But we were standing closely together, almost leaning towards each other. I abandoned my glass and put my arms around her.

It had been a considerable time since I'd had sex with someone and the need in me was great. She seemed to feel the same. But we were in no hurry. I enjoyed the feel and smell of her. Her body was well covered but not soft and when she lifted my hands onto her breasts I felt the smooth silk of her blouse and the fabric of her bra and the firmness underneath. I heard my own sharp intake of breath and kissed her hard. She moved her hand to my crotch and gripped me.

'I want to,' she said. 'You do, too.'

'Yes.'

'Come on.'

She led me through to her bedroom. We took off each other's clothes in a slow-moving dance around the bed. She turned on a lamp. I pulled back the covers. We lay down and rolled together in an embrace that had us touching from head to toe. She was broad-shouldered and wide-hipped. She had the remnants of a deep summer tan except where her swimsuit had been. I kissed her pale breasts and she moaned and stroked me. Her nipples hardened. She opened her legs and I put my hand between them and probed.

'You're not married now, are you?' she said.

'No.'

'I haven't slept with a man for two years. I haven't wanted to.'

I was looking at her face. Her skin was taut over her cheekbones, smooth and clear. I was inside her, feeling the wetness and I knew I was filling her hand. My voice was hoarse. 'Tess, we don't have to fuck if you don't want to. We can do something else.'

She wriggled free of me and reached into a shelf under the bedside table. She held up a packet of condoms. 'You're a vile seducer to say something like that. Fuck me, please.'

Later, she pulled the blankets up and we dozed for a little while, locked close together the way only new lovers can be. Discomfort isn't an issue, only the contact. I felt her stirring and thought she was going to pull away but she didn't.

If anything, she moved closer. I took a firmer hold to show her my appreciation.

'Are you all right?' she murmured.

'I'm a lot better than all right. You?'

'Mm.'

I began to take in details of the room for the first time — polished floor with rug, built-in wardrobes with mirrored doors, heavy curtains. The bed was queen size and low, with wicker bedside tables — one bare, the other holding books, a drinking glass and a lamp. The sheets were some kind of coarse, nubbly cotton. In the dim light I couldn't make out the colour scheme, but I liked the unfussy, spartan feel of the room. It was something like my own bedroom, except that I was inclined to let the empty glasses and coffee mugs build up and the odd sock and T-shirt to lie about.

'Detecting, are you?' she said.

I nuzzled down into her hair for the smell of roses it held. 'Not really. It's just that I was so blinded by lust when I came in that I didn't notice a bloody thing.'

'Controlled lust, I'd say. Whatever happens, I'm glad I broke the drought with you.'

'Likewise, it's been a bit of a drought for me, too. I nearly . . .'

'What?'

'Nothing.'

Now she did pull away, slightly. 'Come on, I thought we were getting close here. I don't want your life story, Cliff. But you were starting to say something about the here and now, weren't you?'

I had a sense that this was one of those crucial

moments when you tell the truth and suffer the consequences, or don't, and feel things slip way from you, go out of your control because you didn't have the guts.

'The other day I tracked Damien Talbot to an address in Homebush. He'd left. The woman who told me this was a prostitute. She had your leaflet about Tadpole Creek. She was at least my age, maybe older.'

'You were tempted?'

I nodded. 'She was a nice woman.'

She moved back to where she'd been before and her hand got busy again. 'Use it or lose it,' she said. 'So I got lucky and she didn't make a sale.'

I laughed, and the feeling that I could do a lot of laughing with this woman excited me almost as much as the smooth, warm skin of her shoulders and what she was doing to me. We made love again.

After, we lay close together with only the film of sweat on our bodies separating us. She raised herself up on one elbow and kissed me in what felt like an exploratory fashion.

'You've been drinking.'

'Yep. Whisky, very good Irish whisky in fact. With a woman.'

'Oh.'

'Nice woman. Very small.'

'Yes?'

'Older than me.'

'How much older?'

'Oh, I'd say thirty-five years, give or take a few.'

She dropped back and I rolled over and I took her breasts in my hands, drew them together and kissed the nipples.

'When I was young they didn't need lifting up.'

'They don't need much now. When I was young I'd be getting ready for you again pretty soon. Come to think of it . . .'

'What?'

I told her about the impotence clinic and she laughed until she ran out of breath. Then she stopped laughing and looked at me seriously.

'I didn't realise just how far you're prepared to go in your work. I shouldn't have objected when you questioned me that way. You can't help it, can you?'

'I could've been more subtle.'

'Bugger subtlety. A man's dead, a dangerous bastard's on the loose and you've still got to find this girl for your poor ex-wife — and for yourself, if you'd just be honest about it. I want to help. No restrictions. I mean it.'

'Okay. Have you got any of that good plonk to hand and an egg or two?'

'I think I can manage something a bit better than that. Where the hell did my knickers finish up?'

I got dressed, Tess put on a black kimono and pretty soon we were sitting in the kitchen eating microwaved lasagne and drinking Jacob's Creek red. She'd also made a salad out of what she called the wreckage of her vegetable garden. Mindful of how touchy she'd been the time before, I ate and drank appreciatively and didn't jump straight in.

She grinned at me. 'Okay, you've shown enough restraint for now. Ask away.'

'I want to talk to Ramsay to see if he can help me find Talbot. Can you tell me where he's likely to be?'

'Yes.' She looked at her wrist and grinned again when she realised she hadn't put her watch back on. Neither had I. I guessed that we both had the same thought: *Was I staying the night?* She fetched her watch from the bedroom. 'He'll be here around ten. He's going to tell me what went on with the TV interview.'

'D'you think he'd know anything about Talbot that he wouldn't tell the police?'

Tess took a mouthful, chewed and swallowed and washed it down with some red. 'Possibly. Ramsay's an anarchist. He's got no time for the police. The question is, if he *does* know anything, would he tell you?'

This was tricky territory. How do brothers feel about their sister's lovers? I hadn't met any of the men my sister had known at uni before she was engaged and swiftly married, so I had no experience in the area.

Tess seemed amused. 'I can read your mind,' she said. 'Will Ramsay be so upset if he knows we're fucking that he won't talk to you?'

'Will he?'

'Probably. He'd have strong doubts about you, seeing that you're a lackey of the capitalist establishment. That's one thing.'

145

She got up, came around behind me and locked me to the chair with her arms. 'I don't *think* you're a shit, are you? You're not just using me to get information.'

I let my head drop back until I could feel it pressing against her breasts, loose under the kimono. 'Not at all. I went to sleep thinking about you the other night and I thought about you through the day. I was very glad when you rang, Tess.'

She kissed the top of my head. 'Still thick on top, very thick. That's nice.' She let go and returned to her seat. 'Okay. We'll have a go at him together. If he does have any clues about getting on to Talbot we'll find out. Might be best if I got dressed, not that he won't be able to tell. You've got such an apres sex look on you.'

'You too.'

We finished the food and most of the bottle. Tess showered and put on white jeans, medium heels and a black velvet blouse. Despite what she'd said she seemed a bit nervous about her brother's visit. She tidied things until I stopped her. I kissed her and held her against me.

'Like that, is it?' she said.

'Like that.'

'Good. Oh, that's good.'

We kissed hard and when we let go she laughed and did a few dance steps. 'You make me feel so young,' she crooned in a very fair Sinatra impersonation.

'If you want me to join in with spring is sprung and so on, forget it. I sing as flat as a tack.'

146

'Maybe you could be taught. Coffee?'

As she was making the coffee she said, 'You know it's a funny thing. There was a kid down at the site today asking questions about us. Sort of, I don't know, questions like you might ask, or did ask.'

Well, we were at it now. In this business, no matter how hard you try, if you get emotionally involved with one of the players, there comes a time when you have to choose between being honest with the person and the requirements of the investigation. It usually comes out the same way. I kept my voice neutral. 'A kid?'

She busied herself with the coffee. 'Yeah. Nice looking youngster. I mean, twenty or so. The girls took to him.'

I hesitated. Show too much interest and her suspicions could be aroused, too little likewise. *Think of something neutral, Cliff and do it quickly.*

I was saved by a noise outside. Tess finished with the percolator and smoothed back her hair. 'That's Ramsay. I can hear that beat-up old Honda of his a mile away. I'll just go and turn on the front porch light.'

She brushed against me as she left the kitchen and I stood listening to the percolator, wishing that I could be totally honest with her.

18

Ramsay Hewitt, standing a full head taller, followed his sister into the kitchen

'You remember Cliff Hardy,' Tess said.

Hewitt did remember. He didn't like the memory and he didn't like what he was seeing now. His craggy, but somehow spoiled-looking face, arranged itself in something close to a scowl. 'What's he doing here?'

'He's looking for Damien and Megan. I've been trying to help him.'

Hewitt shrugged out of his bomber jacket and threw it at a chair. It only half-caught but that was apparently enough for him. He looked at Tess, then at me. His expression was hard to judge. 'I don't think you should have anything to do with him. Jesus, Tessie . . .'

'Don't call me that! I've told you not to call me that!'

I had the feeling that I was witnessing something more than a brother and sister spat. These people were well into adulthood but their behaviour was childish with some sort of edge.

I'd left my holstered pistol over a chair not far

from where Hewitt's jacket hung. My jacket was covering it and I thought I could remove gun and jacket without exposing it. I moved towards the chair. 'Perhaps I'd better go, Tess.'

She moved abruptly into my path. 'No! You're being stupid, Ramsay. You're tired out after what you've been through. Calm down and have a drink.'

'That's your solution for everything,' he said sulkily. But he let Tess pour him some wine and set it down in front of him.

'Cliff?'

'The coffee's done,' I said. 'I'd like some of that.' I looked at Hewitt. 'With a splash of Scotch if you've got any.'

Hewitt was watching us closely and I suppose he could tell the way things were. A halfway intelligent person usually can. I decided to make it easier for him to react by moving close to Tess while she poured the coffee, opening the cupboard at her direction and adding whisky to both our cups.

We sat at the table. 'Snap out of it, Ramsay. Tell us about the night in the lockup.'

Us, she said. Hewitt drank some wine and looked resentful but resigned. I guessed that his wish to talk about himself overrode his other feelings. 'It was interesting,' he said. 'Being deprived of your liberty. Powerful stuff.'

'You should try it long term,' I said.

He looked at me with something that might have been respect if it hadn't been filtered through dislike. 'You've been inside?'

'On remand for a few months in the Bay years

back, and I did a short stint at Berrima not so long ago.'

'Yeah? What for?'

I shrugged and drank some of the laced coffee. 'Oh, destroying evidence and generally pissing off the police.'

'All very interesting,' Tess said. 'What about the TV interview?'

The spoiled look came back again. 'You didn't see it?'

I'd forgotten all about it, but Tess came to the rescue.

'I taped it. I was waiting for you to come and watch it and tell me how it went and how much they edited.'

Me, this time, not us. I was beginning to get an idea of how Ramsay felt about his sister, the question for me was: were the feelings reciprocated? I'd been in this particular neck of the woods before.

'Well, let's see it,' Hewitt said. 'And I'll tell you.'

He was happy now and, without actually including me, wasn't positively leaving me out. Afterall, he was going to be the star of the show. Nothing competes with television, especially not reality.

Tess glanced at me. I kept my expression just on the right side of neutral. I *did* want to see the tape. We trooped into the living room and Tess hit the buttons. They left their drinks behind; I topped myself up from the bottle. Seating arrangements were straightforward. Ramsay on the two-seater couch; me on a chair; Tess between us.

150

The program presenter, a glossy blonde in a severely tailored suit with a very short skirt, crossed her legs and sailed in: 'Tonight, in the studio we have Ramsay Hewitt, the leader . . .'

'Excuse me. Everyone involved in the Tadpole Creek protest is a leader, or there's no leader. Have it whichever way you like.'

She didn't miss a beat. 'I see. Ramsay Hewitt of the Homebush protest . . .'

'Tadpole Creek environmental protest.'

'Right. Ramsay is here to explain the tragic event of the other night and . . .'

Ramsay got out of his chair and advanced on the camera. 'I'm not here to do any such thing. I'm here to tell the viewers about what's being done at Homebush Bay. How they're being conned into thinking that these are going to be green Olympics whereas in fact they're going to be dirty brown . . .'

The camera panned quickly back to the presenter. To be fair to her, she was coping well with her obstreperous guest. 'Red, wouldn't you say, Ramsay? Blood red? That man was beaten to death.'

A floor attendant shepherded Ramsay back to his seat. He combed his long hair back with his fingers. He was good-looking or would have been but for a nervous, twitchy manner that seemed to affect his facial expressions and bodily movements. He bore some resemblance to his sister and would've looked more like her still if he survived another ten years and managed to resolve some of his all too apparent inner conflicts. 'I'm very sorry about the guard,' he said slowly. 'It shouldn't have happened.'

'But it did. What can you tell us about . . .,' the presenter's eyes flickered to a cue card, '. . .Damien Talbot?'

'Every organisation has rotten apples.'

The presenter leaned forward. 'Would you like to expand on that, Ramsay?'

'Yes.' He broke off and reached for a glass of water. 'I mean the police, the church, the media, they all have unworthy people in them, don't they? I'd much rather talk about what the protest is designed to do.'

The presenter felt herself to be on top now and she showed signs of knowing that she'd presided over a pretty good short grab and that it was time to close off. 'I'm sure you would, but what I want to know is why would one of your people behave so violently?'

'I don't consider him to be a member of the group.'

'So there's division within the protest. That's not going to help your cause, is it?'

Ramsay didn't answer.

'What can you tell us about the young woman with him — Megan French?'

'Nothing. I scarcely knew her.'

'I see what you mean about the protest having no leader. Maybe it should have had one. I'm Tracey-Jane Marshall and this is *Newsbeat*.'

A commercial followed and then the tape stopped. It was a lame performance from Ramsay who was clearly out of his depth. He didn't seem to realise it and looked at Tess for her approval. When he didn't get it he wet his lips and fidgeted in his seat. 'That bloody bitch set me up. Her questions weren't fair.'

No questions would ever be fair for Ramsay, he was one of those people who found something or someone else to blame at every turn.

Tess said, 'Well, it'll be forgotten tomorrow. What we have to do is . . .'

Ramsay jumped from his seat and stood over her. 'You seem to have forgotten bloody everything. Everything except screwing with this fascist thug . . .'

He was working himself up to do something, anything, to relieve his frustration, even if it meant hitting Tess. I moved quickly and grabbed his flailing arm.

'Take it easy, Ramsay. Get a grip on yourself or you'll do something you're sorry for.'

For all his size he wasn't strong and it was child's play to get him off balance. He sensed that he had no leverage to resist me and it made him even wilder and less effective. He stumbled and almost fell into Tess's lap. I hauled him upright and he sprayed spittle as he shook himself free.

'You slut! Screw your brains out. See if I care. I don't need you. Go to hell.' He stormed back to the kitchen and swore as he hit something solid. Then the back door crashed open against the wall and I heard his boots on the cement path at the side of the house. Tess was huddled in the chair with her face in her hands. I was torn. I still wanted to talk to Ramsay but Tess's distress was strong and visible. I knelt by the chair and stroked her head. I heard an engine start, run roughly and then a squeal of tyres as he drove away. Tess heard it all as well and felt it more — her body shook at the sounds. When she looked up there was a pain in her eyes and expression that was hard to watch.

'I'm sorry about all that,' she said.

'He's got troubles.'

'You know, don't you?'

'What?'

'The . . . the nature of his troubles.'

I knew all right, from the way he looked at her and behaved, but I said, 'I'm not sure that it's my business.'

She sucked in a deep breath. 'Perhaps you're right. Look, Cliff, I'm whacked. I'm going to take half a pill and go to sleep. I'd be glad if you'd just stick around until I'm off. Would you mind?'

It was a subtle request. I topped up my coffee and added another drop of Scotch while she got ready for bed.

'Lock the door, would you, Cliff. Key goes in the flower pot.'

Dark red silk pyjamas, a scrubbed face, a slightly toothpaste-flavoured kiss and she was gone. After a while, I went into the bedroom and looked at her. She'd turned over and drawn her legs up and seemed comfortable. I had an impulse to strip off and crawl in beside her but I knew that wasn't what she wanted. Just as well I didn't because when I was putting my jacket on the mobile rang.

154

I answered, keeping my voice down.

'Cliff, this is Geoff. Mum's in hospital. It looks pretty bad. I'll get back to you when I can.'

19

I didn't know what hospital Cyn would be in and with family gathering round it wouldn't be appropriate for me to be there anyway. I was tired and somewhat dispirited. Ramsay Hewitt's abrupt departure had closed off an avenue of enquiry. I doubted whether Geoff had picked up anything useful at the protest site. It was possible and that it had been put out of his mind by his mother's crisis, but it seemed unlikely. If I'd had the manpower I might've staked out Dr Macleod's compound to see if Talbot turned up there, but I didn't, and there was no real reason to think he would.

I checked on Tess again, followed her instructions about the key and left the house. There was nothing for me to do but go home. I felt sober, very sober, but I might have been over the limit. I thought back over what I'd eaten and drunk in the past few hours and decided it was line ball. I drove sedately and caught a late night news bulletin on the way. The police were still hunting what the media were now calling 'the Tadpole Creek Killer'. I was working at the centre of one of the city's major news items but felt that I was on the sidelines with no chance of getting into the game.

I turned into my street and cursed when I saw that my usual parking space outside the house was occupied by another car. Inner city dwellers tend to establish conventions and protocols about these things and it was rare for one of the other residents to pinch my spot. The occasional visitor or Glebe diner-out offends, but they were usually gone by this time. I parked further down the street and walked back with the gun in its holster under my jacket.

As I approached the house a woman came out of my neighbour's place and walked smartly towards the red hatchback parked in what I considered my spot. I stopped and watched her and she stopped and looked at me. I guessed I must've looked threatening at that time of night with the experience of the last few hours showing on my face and a suspicious package under my arm

'It's okay,' I said. 'I live next door to Clive. My name's Hardy. We're mates.'

Relief was apparent in every muscle in her body. 'Oh, the private detective. Clive's told me about you. Oh God, I've taken your space.'

'Don't worry,' I said. 'I won't shoot you.'

She laughed. 'I should hope not. Sorry again. There was a van pulling out from here when I arrived. I didn't know it was your spot.'

'Only by convention,' I said. 'First come, first served really.'

'Well, I'll be off. Goodnight, Mr Hardy.'

'Goodnight.' I stood, debating whether to move my car as she pulled neatly away and drove off. Clive is a taxi driver and we both keep irregular hours and live alone. The woman who'd left was thirtyish, about Clive's age, and attractive. *Good luck to you*, I thought. *And good luck to me, too*. I'd decided to leave the car where it was when I saw Clive standing at his gate and beckoning to me.

I wasn't in the mood for conversation, but I was always ready to give Clive the time of day or more usually, night.

'Gidday, Clive.'

'Cliff. Look, it's probably nothing, but there was a strange-looking van parked outside your place briefly when Sally arrived. I didn't think anything of it at first. You've had that other young bloke staying. Thought it must've been to do with something you're working on. But he gave me a funny look and drove off like a hoon.'

'What d'you mean, strange looking?'

'All colours of the rainbow — pyschedelic. What's wrong?'

My brain snapped on the connections: *van — psychedelic design — Damien Talbot*. He'd been here!

The tiredness had dropped away as I felt a reaction rise inside me I hadn't experienced for a long time — that of the hunter becoming the hunted. 'Tall bloke? Long hair?'

'That's him. Anything wrong?'

'No, mate. Probably not. How long was he here?'

158

'In and out I'd say. Well, I've gotta clean up and start my shift. 'Night, Cliff.'

My security is reasonably good. The front door is a solid job, deadlocked. The house is free-standing on one side but the bougainvillea grows so thickly in the front that you'd lose a hell of a lot of skin trying to get through. At the back is a drop of a couple of metres to the lane and there are a couple of blocks of flats opposite with windows looking out. Hard to break into. All clear there. I inspected the front porch as best I could in the dim light but there didn't appear to be anything of concern — no suspicious parcels, no bodies.

I unlocked the door, turned on the light and saw the sheet of paper that had been slipped under the door. I closed the door behind me and picked it up.

LEAVE ME ALONE OR I'LL FUCKING
KILL HER!!!

Capitals in heavy black Texta on a sheet of quarto copy paper.

The adrenaline rush that had hit me outside ebbed away and I felt bone-tired. The 'her' had to be Megan and I had no idea of where to look for her. I dropped the holster on a chair, stripped off my jacket and went to the bathroom where I washed my face and hands. I drank three glasses of water and made coffee, keeping my mind a blank. When the coffee was ready I drank half a cup scalding hot and refilled it, then went through to look at the paper again and think.

What if the 'her' referred to in the note wasn't Megan French? Bad images were jumping around in my head: sick women, dead women, women sleeping or maybe dead. *Tess.*

I swallowed a couple of high-octane caffeine tablets, grabbed my gun and jacket and raced out to the car. I headed back towards Tess Hewitt's house without any of the caution I'd employed before. If Talbot knew where I lived and where Tess lived what was to stop him hurting her?

With the caffeine kicking in I drove too fast and badly, narrowly missing other cars and shrieking around bends on tortured tyres. I didn't care and I was lucky there were no cops on the road and that I didn't encounter anyone as out of control as me. I pulled up outside Tess's house and sprinted for the verandah, stumbling on the path and almost falling up the steps. I clawed the key out of the flowerpot where I'd left it, unlocked the door and strode through to the bedroom with my heart thundering in my chest and my vision blurred.

She was there. A curled-up shape in the centre of the big bed. One arm lay outside the bed-clothes and her other hand was clenched and near her mouth. In my hectic state I didn't quite believe it. I bent down to make sure I could hear her breathing and only eased back when I heard it and saw the slow rise and fall of her body under the blanket. I must have made some noise because she stirred and changed position. She muttered something I couldn't catch and then settled back into untroubled sleep.

160

I was sweating from a combination of emotional reaction and chemical disturbance as I backed out of the bedroom. My mouth was sandpaper dry. I went into the kitchen and filled a glass with water and drank it. The Scotch bottle was sitting beside the sink and I poured myself a generous measure and added a little water. I took the drink into the living room and dropped into an easy chair.

I drank the whisky and checked on Tess again. Then I drank more whisky and did another check. I told myself I was there to protect her but I was really there for the comfort of her presence. I acknowledged that just before I fell asleep to the sound of falling rain.

20

'Cliff. Cliff. Are you all right? What're you doing here?'

Tess shook me awake from an uneasy sleep that left me with half-remembered dreams and an all-too present crick in my neck. I struggled to the surface and found her standing over me wrapped in her kimono with her hair standing up, tear stains in the remains of yesterday's makeup. She still looked good and I stood creakily and put my arms around her.

'It was a hell of a night,' I said. 'Things happened after you went to sleep and I had to come back to make sure you were all right.'

'What things?'

'Let me get cleaned up and I'll tell you.' I was reluctant to let her go and she didn't seem to want me to. I smoothed down her hair. 'I'm sorry about Ramsay. I'm very sorry. I feel partly responsible.'

She released herself, backed off and looked at me. 'What d'you mean?'

'I mean if I hadn't started poking around things might not have turned out like this. Probably wouldn't have.'

She shook her head. 'No. This goes back before you. Both things — me and Ramsay and the protest. I knew there was something wrong about the Tadpole Creek protest and about Damien Talbot. But the thing had given Ramsay a focus and me too for that matter, and I didn't want to admit it. You're not responsible, Cliff. Don't think that. Have a shower. Ramsay left some shaving stuff here, I think, before he started growing the beard. I'll make coffee.'

I showered and shaved using one of Ramsay's disposable razors and a cake of soap. The razor had been used before and soap doesn't make the best lather. I avoided nicking myself but the result was pretty rough. I tamed my hair with Tess's brush, but there was nothing I could do about a shirt that had been sweated into, made wet with tears and slept in.

In the kitchen Tess pointed to the coffee pot and a plate of buttered toast and went off to the bathroom. I was feeling seedy and hungover from the Scotch and the caffeine of the night before so I did the only thing possible. I poured the last dregs of the whisky into an inch of black coffee and slugged it down. Then I poured a full mug, added milk and drank it with sugar and three slices of toast. Then I had another mug. It was the most liquids and solids I'd taken in for breakfast in years and I have to admit that it made me feel better.

Tess came in wearing a dark dress and low heels. She'd put on her makeup and her hair was still wet but brushed so that it'd dry into a neat, slightly severe, shape around her head. With a start I realised that she bore a resemblance to Helen Broadway, a lover of some years ago. That relationship hadn't turned out well and I pushed the thought away. She poured herself some coffee and cut a piece of toast into small squares.

'I saw the gun,' she said.

I'd left it on a chair in the living room meaning to put my jacket over it. I nodded.

'Tell me what's happened.' she said.

I told her about Talbot being at my place and the note and my uncertainty about whether the note had referred to Megan French or her. I told her about Macleod and Miss Cartwright's accusations and the connection with Talbot. She drank coffee, nibbled toast and listened without responding. I still didn't tell her about my attempt to infiltrate the protest group with Geoff Samuels. I felt bad about it, but I couldn't think of a way to make it look right. I finished talking, ate some more toast and drank some more coffee.

'You have to go to the police,' Tess said.

'It wouldn't do any good. They don't know where to find Talbot any more than I do. And I haven't got enough to make the police even knock on Macleod's door.'

'I wonder if Ramsay knows anything about Talbot and this doctor. He and Damien were close at first, or so it seemed. Until they had a falling out over tactics and . . . leadership.'

'That was one of the things I was going to ask him last night, before he blew his stack.'

'And what else?'

I fingered an irritating patch of stubble I'd

missed with the blunt razor. 'I suppose about Megan. He told the interviewer that he hardly knew her. D'you think that's true?'

Tess was slow to answer. 'We're getting to it, aren't we?'

'Getting to what?'

'C'mon, Cliff. You're not that dumb. You saw how Ramsay is with me, about me. Isn't there something you want to ask?'

'No. Is there something you want to tell me?'

She gave it serious thought, then snapped her fingers. 'Okay. Why not? I worked it all out with a therapist a long time ago. I've moved on. I'm ten years older than Ramsay. As I said, I looked after him from the time he was fifteen, when our parents died. He took it very hard. He was very close to Mum. Inconsolable. One night he came into my bed. Remember I was young, too and trying to cope with grief *and* responsibility. Anyway, it happened. A few times. Then we stopped. I thought I'd got through it without damage and I pretty much did. As I say, I got some help later. Ramsay didn't get through it and he's refused to discuss it, let alone have therapy. I don't know anything about his sex life now. I don't think he has one.'

I nodded and scratched at the stubble.

'Your reaction?'

'Admiration for you, sympathy for him.'

She put her arms around me. 'Thanks. Look, I'm going to have to try to get in touch with him, calm him down. You understand?'

'Yes, of course.'

165

'I'll try to get him to talk to you. Might be hard.'

'Okay. I should go and check on a few things. See if there's anything I've missed that might go somewhere.'

'I've got all your numbers, mate. I'll track you down.'

I wondered if she meant it.

21

For no good reason I drove to the Homebush site and stopped at a point where I could see a lot of the activity. Maybe it was my imagination, but I thought I could see progress in just those few days. Staying clear of the security posts, I drove as close as I could get to the Tadpole Creek protest. There were fewer people around and one corner of the banner had broken free of its mooring and drooped down. It had the look of a show about to fold. I ran my eye along the unimpressive, sluggish little watercourse with its few scruffy mangroves and general air of insignificance. It was hard to tell what purpose the area on the protesters' side of the creek had served before their arrival. Part playground, part rubbish dump perhaps.

The rain hadn't amounted to much and the sky was rapidly clearing. From my vantage point I could see back towards Concord and Tess's neighbourhood. I wondered what she'd meant about knowing there was something not right about the protest and why I hadn't asked her. I wasn't displaying my best form and I knew why.

I was worried about failing Cyn, worried about the young woman who might be my daughter and caught up in a relationship that might or might not go somewhere. Too many cross-currents for efficient work.

Back in the car, I fingered the irritating patch of stubble and felt like a drink, like several drinks. I was thinking seriously about a visit to the former Sheep Shit Inn when the mobile rang. My first thought was of Tess and I grabbed the phone.

'Tess?'

'This is Geoff Samuels, Cliff.'

'Oh, Geoff, right. How is she?'

'Not good, but she got through the night and they think she can pull up a bit. She doesn't really want to except for this business about Megan French. She wants to see you, Cliff.'

'Okay. Where are you?'

He named a private hospital in Willoughby and I said I'd be there as quickly as I could.

'I should warn you that my sister's here. Annie. Mum was muttering something about Megan and Annie's latched onto it. She wants to know everything. I've stalled her. I'm afraid I've sort of lumbered you with it. Annie's always had the edge on me. I thought you could handle it better.'

'Well, I'll do what I can.'

'The thing is, she knows all about you. Has for a long time. Apparently she found some letters or something Mum had. You're not her favourite person, Cliff.'

'Great. See you soon.'

I forgot about alcohol and headed towards

Willoughby. As I drove I thought of the time Cyn and I had spent together. Mostly, I remembered the fights and the silences and it was hard to say which were the worst. The big silence was coming and it was beginning to look as if I'd let her down, again.

Propped up against pillows, wearing a white cotton nightgown with a high neck, Cyn looked shrunken to half her proper size. I tried to arrange my face so as to conceal the waves of shock, sympathy and sadness that washed over me but, sick as she was, she could still read me accurately.

'Pretty bad, huh,' she said in a surprisingly strong voice. 'Fact is that it's worse for all of you than it is for me.'

I approached the bed and took her hand briefly. I couldn't speak. Geoff was sitting in a chair by the window and a woman a few years older than him, but bearing a strong physical resemblance, sat close by the bed.

'This is my daughter, Anne, Cliff.'

She returned my nod. 'Anne Samuels,' she said. 'How do you do?'

She was good-looking and well dressed — dark, layer-cut hair, expert makeup, blue blouse and business suit, minimal jewellery. No sign of her pregnancy yet. No sign of a wedding ring either. A modern woman. She looked intelligent and tough, not a common combination and that sharp nod spoke volumes. Anne Samuels looked as if she thought it'd be a good idea to push me out the window, and we were ten storeys up.

'I want you to explain things to Anne. About Megan. Try to make her understand. I haven't the strength.'

I didn't know that I had the ability, but I nodded.

Cyn drew in a deep breath. The neck of the nightgown gaped and I could see that she was wasted to skin and bone. Her eyes seemed unnaturally large in her shrunken face. 'How far have you got, Cliff? Tell me the truth.'

I shook my head. 'Not far, Cyn. There's a few things to follow up on but it takes time.'

'Time's just exactly what I haven't got. No, scrub that. I'm determined to hang on until you find her.'

I heard Anne Samuels' angry snort but Cyn, if she heard it, ignored the response. 'Geoff tells me you took him to see a prostitute.'

'A very nice prostitute,' Geoff said.

Cyn's smile was full and bright and convinced me that she wasn't at her last gasp yet.

'That's right,' I said.

With an effort, Cyn stirred on the pillows and although it evidently caused her pain, she moved her shrivelled upper body minimally to left and right. 'He's a good boy, and Anne's a good girl. I just need to know about the other one as well.'

Geoff had spent enough time with her to know the signs. He touched her hand. 'You're tired, Mum. Better get some rest.'

Cyn nodded. She was hooked up to several bottles with various tubes running into her. At a guess, morphine was on tap. Her eyelids fluttered.

Geoff kissed her on the cheek. After a brief hesitation, Anne did the same and we left the room.

Outside, Anne fronted me like a footballer getting in an opponent's face. She was surprisingly tall, not much shorter than her brother. 'I want to talk to you but I need a cigarette first.'

'There's a smoking area down here, Annie,' Geoff said quietly. 'But should you be smoking now that you're . . .'

'Shut up. I'd quit before this happened. You can have a joint and maybe get up the courage to deal with this arsehole.'

We went down the corridor and out onto a small balcony. Anne took out a packet of filters and lit up. She exhaled and some of the smoke drifted my way. I was somewhere between annoyed and amused. She was genuinely aggressive but working at it as well and her acting wasn't quite up to the job. I made allowances for the fact that her mother was dying and didn't let it get to me. Not too much.

'You're exploiting her.'

I shook my head. 'No.'

'I know all about you. What an arsehole you were when you and Mum were married.'

'It was a bad marriage,' I said. 'But pretty much a fair fight.'

She puffed hard. 'You shit! You glib shit.'

'Easy, Annie,' Geoff said.

She spun around. 'Easy yourself. *Geoffrey*. You ought to be shot, going along with this crap. Can't you see that this man's conning her? Taking advantage of . . .'

After the events of the last few hours that was a bit too much. I moved forward and snatched the cigarette from her hand and threw it into one of the big ashtrays. I grabbed her arm, pulled her off balance and pushed her down into a chair. I stood over her.

'You just listen to me, young lady. You couldn't be more wrong. Your mother thinks this Megan French is her daughter. My daughter, too. I don't know and for my part I don't care much. I'm not a family type. But it matters to Cyn in the last days of her life and that's what matters to me. And to Geoff, too. And if you had any decency in you you'd see that and not give a shit about anything else but helping her to die in peace. That's what Cyn wants and you should too, and fuck any other fucking selfish ideas you might have in your fucking selfish yuppie head.'

She looked up at me and the veneer of toughness and sophistication fell away. Her shoulders started to move, her eyes brimmed and overflowed and then she was weeping and her body was shaken by deep, racking sobs. Geoff knelt beside her and put one arm awkwardly around her shoulders. She leaned towards him and they held each other in a strained, uncomfortable pose that made me feel like crying as well.

We went to the hospital coffee shop and sat and talked for half an hour while Anne calmed down. She admitted that she had a big load of guilt resulting from some years of conflict with her mother.

172

'And now it's too late to make it up to her.'

'I doubt that she sees it that way,' I said.

'She doesn't.' Geoff had one of his joints going but there are all sorts of strange smells in hospitals. 'She just says you take after Dad, and remember how they used to fight sometimes. But they still . . .'

'Loved each other. Yes, I know. I'm sorry to expose you to all this, Mr Hardy. A couple of years back we were really quite a normal family.'

'It's okay. You've had a bad run.'

'And it's not over yet. Geoff, I'm going to stay here. They have rooms for support persons as they call them. That's one thing I can do. That'll take some pressure off you.'

Geoff nodded. 'What about your job?'

'Fuck them.'

'I never thought I'd hear you say that.'

'This stuff helps you get things in perspective.' She lit a cigarette and looked at me. 'I don't fully understand what you're doing, Mr Hardy. I . . .'

'Cliff,' I said. 'To tell you the truth I'm at a bit of a loss myself at this point. You know that Megan French is with this Talbot kid. He's bloody dangerous.'

Anne puffed and looked ready to go on the attack again. 'What about *her*, is *she* dangerous?'

'I don't know.' I told them about my meeting with Megan's parents and the impression I'd formed of them. They expressed sympathy, but neither was really in a state to relate much to other people's problems.

Geoff butted his joint and pocketed the roach. 'Tell you one thing, I found out a bit about that land at Tadpole Creek — past owners and that. Shit, I've forgotten, but a name came up that we've run into before.' He rubbed his face. 'I'm too whacked to remember. It's on the printouts at your house.'

I pushed my chair back and stood. 'Geoff's staying at my place while we work on this, Anne. Have you got everything you need here?'

She forced a smile. 'Really looking after us aren't you? Our mother's first husband.'

'I'm trying,' I said.

Geoff had his own car at the hospital and we drove in convoy back to Glebe with me easily keeping him in sight. That was unusual. Being young, he normally drove faster than me as I'd seen, even in the rain which was falling heavily now. It looked as if his mother's plight had slowed him down in every way. Understandable, but it could limit his usefulness. I hoped he wouldn't increase the dope to tobacco ratio in his smokes.

I showed him the note Talbot had left. It jolted him out of the passive state he appeared to be slipping into.

'Jesus, he's crazy. I talked to a few people at the site and that's the impression I got. He's a scary guy.'

I wanted to question him more closely on that but he bounded up the stairs. 'I want to show you these printouts.'

I followed him, expecting to hear the sound of the computer being turned on and the rustle of paper. Instead I found him in the doorway to the room. He was pale and leaning against the archi-trave for support.

'What's wrong?' I said.

'It's all gone. The computer, the printer, the disks, the lot. All gone.'

I brushed past him into the room. The desk that had been covered with computer equipment and accessories was bare. The wastepaper basket was empty. The place had been swept clean, profes-sionally. Geoff pushed off from the door jamb and looked as if he'd like to take a swing at me.

'Some private eye you are. Some bloody secu-rity you've got here. Fuck it. That was my computer.'

I said nothing and went downstairs. I examined the locks on the back and front doors. Not a sign of forced entry. This had been done by someone who knew how to do it and had the equipment. Not Talbot, he hadn't been here long enough and had no real reason. Macleod? Possible, but again, although he might be alarmed at my making a connection between him and Talbot, he had no reason to go this far. Millennium Security seemed like the best bet. I went into the kitchen and poured myself a glass of wine.

Geoff wandered in and sneered. 'That'd be right. Go for the grog.'

'Take it easy, Geoff. This was a super smooth professional job. They'd have got past practically any security system. I'm sorry about your com-puter but I've got full insurance and . . .'

'Fuck that. I had stuff on the hard disk I need.'

I'd had enough of members of the Samuels

family getting up my nose. 'Too bad. You should've backed it up on floppies. I thought you computer nerds knew all about that.'

He took it to heart. 'I'm not a computer nerd,' he muttered.

'I know. I'm sorry. Look, we're both on edge and you look like you didn't get much sleep last night.'

'I didn't.'

'Me either.' I got some cheese out of the fridge and a loaf from the bread bin. 'Have a drink and something to eat or roll yourself a joint. We've got some serious talking to do. You're young. I hope you've got a young person's memory.'

He must've realised how long it'd been since he'd eaten because he attacked the loaf and the lump of cheese and accepted the glass of wine I poured for him. 'I've got a great memory,' he said with his mouth full. 'I can name the entire cast list of all the *Star Wars* movies.'

'Great, but this could be tougher. What did you get from the Net on Tadpole Creek? I don't expect chapter and verse . . .'

'What does that mean?'

'Never mind. Try to remember everything you can.'

He sat at the table, munched on his bread and cheese and drank his wine. I did the same standing up. *Of course the kid's right*, I thought. *I should've installed a proper security system here years ago.* From that thought I jumped to thinking about the office. At least things were a bit more secure there, but more as a result of a recent

176

renovation of the building than my doing. I knew I'd been slack and didn't like the feeling.

Geoff rolled a joint and lit it. 'I was hacking into recent land transfer registers for the area,' he said. 'It's not hard to do if you know how. That Tadpole Creek land was acquired by the State Government as part of their plans for the Olympics. But there was some kind of bullshit about it. Some sort of protest from the owner. It's still not completely settled and that's the legal basis for the protest. I mean, the government says it is settled and the former owner says it isn't.'

'That's interesting. And who is this former owner?'

'That's the thing I can't quite ... I know we've heard the name.'

I got my notebook and began reading out names as I flipped over the pages. 'Talbot, French, Annette, Hewitt, Smith, Kamenka, Macleod ...'

'That's it! Macleod. The owner was a Dr Bruce Macleod.'

You didn't have to be Stephen Hawking to grasp the significance of that. Dr Macleod, he of the disappearing elderly citizens, was protecting a patch of barren ground by financing an environmental protest and using one of his patients, Damien Talbot, as a stirrer and front man. The inference was obvious — Dr Macleod didn't want the ground to be disturbed.

I explained this to Geoff who took it in but displayed some indifference. I assumed that this was because he was still grieving over the loss of his computer, but he surprised me. He said, 'It doesn't get us any closer to finding Megan French, does it?'

He was right there and I was feeling desperate and frustrated, entertaining notions of locating Ramsay Hewitt and shaking anything he might know out of him or confronting Macleod and his heavies with what little ammunition I had and bluffing him. Just thinking about them made both ideas seem weak. The phone rang and I grabbed it.

'Tess?' I hadn't told Geoff anything about Tess and I saw the interested look on his face before he politely left the room.

'Mr Hardy? This is Dora French.'

I gripped the phone so hard my hand cramped and I had to change hands and wriggle the fingers. 'Yes, Mrs French?'

'I'm in Katoomba. I've managed to get away from the others and Rex for a few minutes but I must talk quickly. I've seen a newspaper report about Megan. We don't have radio or television or papers at Mount Wilson so I didn't know anything about this dreadful trouble Megan's in. I saw a paper in the Ladies' here quite by accident.'

'It's very worrying, Mrs French. She may be in serious danger. Damien Talbot . . .'

'Yes, yes, I appreciate that. I can't go to the police, Mr Hardy. If Rex and Pastor John found out I'd be in awful strife. I have to trust you.'

'Trust me with what, Mrs French?'

'I know where Megan will have gone if she needs to hide.'

'Tell me, please.'

178

'There are some old houses down at Scarborough on the south coast this side of Wollongong. Megan used to go down there to stay with friends. They didn't pay any money. They sort of squatted, I think the expression is. Rex was furious about it. He . . .'

'Where are these places, Mrs French?'

'I don't know exactly. All I remember her saying is that they were above the railway line and they'd been condemned because of a landslip. They have terrible rain down there, you know.'

I did know. The Illawarra escarpment was notoriously unstable in heavy rain and there'd been flooding recently. I pressed her for more information but she became flustered and said she had to ring off because 'the others' would be looking for her. She'd had to beg the money for the phone. She pleaded with me to look after Megan if I found her and I promised I would.

I went through to the living room and found Geoff looking out the dirty window at the leaves blowing around outside. The light was dim. A storm was brewing.

'Are you still in on this? Despite the computer?'

'Of course I am.'

'Okay. Go down to the Glebe library and get on the Net. Look up Scarborough, New South Wales and print out everything you can find. News stuff, land use, development plans and maps. Especially maps.'

'Shit, I wish I had my computer.'

'Well, you don't. Get going.'

'What'll you be doing?'

'First, doing something about getting your computer back. Second, getting ready to go down to Scarborough when you come back with the info.'

'Where is it?'

'Not far, son. Not very far.'

22

It took me quite a while to get through to Smith at Millennium Security and as long again to convince him that I could help him in his difficulties with the Tadpole Creek protest. At a price, of course. He didn't admit that it was his people that had taken Geoff's computer. He didn't have to. They had, and we both knew it.

'I know who's behind the protest and why,' I told him. 'I know how you can stop it. I imagine that'd put you in good with the contractors.'

'Perhaps. Well . . .?'

'I want something in return.'

'I'm listening, Hardy.'

'Being who you are, big and respectable and all that, you'd be liaising closely with the police, right?'

'I said I'm listening.'

'I need to know exactly where they are in their search for Damien Talbot. What leads they're following, if any. The thrust of their investigation, as it were.'

'I imagine I could get something like that. What do I get in return?'

'As I said, the end of the protest.'

'That's very vague.'

'Have you got a better offer on the table? Look, Smith, ask around in the game. See if I'm thought of as a bullshit artist.'

He laughed. 'Oh, I already did that. You're seen as someone who plays by his own rules. I have to admit that the word is your rules are generally pretty fair, if slanted your way. But I'd say that was smart.'

'Okay. I'm telling you that I've got what you need and you'll get it in a straight exchange.'

'There might be other ways of getting the information from you.'

'I don't think so and you wouldn't say that if you'd really asked around.'

'Just a feint, Hardy. Just a feint. You're really prepared to destroy the protest? I thought you were pro-greenie.'

'I don't give a shit about the protest. All I care about is getting Megan French away from Talbot. And don't mention her when you talk to the cops unless you have to. Don't mention me either, of course.'

'Of course.' Testy now. 'Any other instructions?'

'Yeah. I want the computer returned. Intact. Plus the disks and printouts. You can keep the stuff from the wastepaper basket.'

'I'll get back to you.'

I was running the risk that he'd go to the cops for his own purposes. Convince them that I was sitting on evidence and information and bring pressure to bear on me in that way. Somehow, I thought not. My run-ins with the law in recent years — resulting in a short prison term, a suspension and a near-suspension — hadn't done me any harm in the circles that matter. If I was seen as a maverick, it was as a maverick who tried to deliver in his client's interest and my guess was that in this instance Smith would class himself as a client.

I was right. He was back on the phone in just under an hour but sounding hesitant. The rain was drumming on the iron roof and I had to ask him to speak up.

'I want you to know that I pushed it pretty far, Hardy. To the limit.'

'Save the advertising. What did you get?'

'In a word, nothing. They're fucked. Talbot's vanished and they don't know where to look. He's been an inner-city type all his life and they've checked those crummy parts street by street. Nothing. Sorry.'

I could've taken exception to his description of my part of Sydney, but it wasn't worth the effort. The result was more or less what I'd expected and, if I admitted it to myself, what I'd hoped. I wanted to go after Talbot without police interference. It seemed the best chance of getting Megan French away without the shit sticking.

'Hardy?'

'I'm here. That's okay. No mention of me or the girl?'

'None.'

'So, what about the computer?'

'Fuck you! What've you got?'

I told him about Macleod and Talbot and about

my visit to Miss Cartwright and the disappearing oldies and Macleod's legal wrangle over the patch of ground. I hinted at the connection between Talbot and Macleod, which was true, and that one of the protesters had doubts about the financial backing they'd had and Talbot's role in the scheme of things. This was sort of true. Smith was underwhelmed.

'Shit, that's all speculation.'

'Look into it. If you work through those print-outs your boys stole you'll get confirmation about Macleod. Look, Smith, he's killed those old people and planted them at Tadpole Creek. He doesn't want the fucking sods turned.'

There was a long pause while he thought about it. When he spoke again his tone was conspira-torial. 'Just say this all checks out and you're right and we have this Macleod by the balls. What's your attitude, given that?'

I knew what he was talking. Deal. Cover up. I thought of Macleod's contemptuous arrogance and of old Miss Cartwright and her violated life. Then I thought of Cyn and Megan French and Geoff and Anne Samuels and the here and now. The living, if only just in Cyn's case.

'I told you,' I said. 'I don't care what you do. I'm out of it. You can orchestrate it anyway you like. You can take all the credit.'

'The computer'll be delivered within twenty hours.'

So I had that much good news for Geoff when he got back with a stack of printouts he'd only just managed to keep dry in the heavy rain. He was pleased, but he'd got caught up in the work he'd done.

'You know this place, do you, Cliff?'

'Well, I've been there.'

'It sounds as if it's sliding into the sea. Wasn't a good idea to build a town there. Not to mention to put in a road and railway. Both got severely damaged in that downpour about this time last year. It's a wonder they didn't lose a couple of houses.'

I spread the printouts on the kitchen table and did a quick run-through. There were a good number of maps, not all of a useful standard. Also, diagrams, environmental impact studies and piles of material to do with a protest about the plan to construct a tunnel to catch stormwater and put it out on the beach. Geoff rolled a joint and flicked through this material.

'This is one of the craziest ideas I've ever heard,' he said. 'Of course the old mine was the source of all the trouble. I mean that's the reason for the town and the road and railway in the first place. They diverted the creeks and tried to control the water flow by artificial means. Hopeless. Then they reckon they can run it all out on the beach. Quite apart from the fact that it won't work, it'll fuck up the marine environment for sure.'

'Why won't it work?'

'The headland they plan to drill through's too fragile. If they blast, Christ knows what'll happen. Plus they've only got a vague idea of where some of the old mine shafts are and what's in them. Remember when some miners drilled through into an old shaft that'd filled up with water? Not long back? Case in point.'

I was interested, but not as interested as in the material about land use, past and present.

'Slip areas?'

Geoff said, 'I highlighted that stuff.'

He'd gone through the survey, classification and rates maps and papers. 'What's this?' I put my finger on one of the maps where he'd made a circle.

'It's an area of slip close to one of the old orchards. A couple of houses more or less fell over and the council resumed the land. Some silly buggers had built over the old watercourses.' He sorted through some newspaper cuttings. 'Apparently, they had some trouble with squatters there a few years ago. The cops cleared them out, but maybe they came back?'

'You're not bad at this,' I said.

23

Geoff called the hospital, spoke to his sister, and shook his head at my enquiry.

'You don't have to come on this,' I said. 'Maybe you should be with Cyn and Anne.'

'No, I'm coming. I want to be able to tell Mum, well, something, anyway.'

Not a ringing endorsement of the course of action, but I respected his judgement. Geoff, in jeans, boots, sweater and bomber jacket was dressed for the job. I put on similar gear and put a few things like a torch, matches, a sheath knife, a camera into a backpack. I looked out the window at the leaking grey sky and picked up a raincoat and a parka. A one-pint hip flask of Scotch into the backpack and the .38 under my arm and we were ready.

The rain seemed to get still harder as soon as I turned on the engine. It fell heavily and steadily and didn't look like letting up. By the time we reached the Princes Highway the gutters were overflowing and my windshield wipers were only just coping. I turned on the radio and caught a news report about a low out to sea that was bringing the rain and throwing four-metre waves onto the eastern suburbs beaches. It was expected to last for twenty-four hours or more.

'Great,' Geoff said. 'Shit, that escarpment cops it hard. It'll be twice as bad as this down there.'

I said, 'Maybe not,' but feared he was right. I decided that it was a plus: if Talbot was holed up in a shack under the escarpment, the rain would keep him there. With any luck he'd be so busy trying to stay dry he wouldn't notice anyone coming up on him. I told Geoff this and he almost sneered at me.

'Know that Clint Eastwood movie where he says to the crim something like, "It's a question of luck and what you have to ask yourself is do you feel lucky?" Well, do you feel lucky, Cliff?'

'Sometimes,' I said. 'Punk.'

He laughed and his mood lifted.

My biggest worry was that the coast road from Stanwell Park would be closed and that I'd be forced to go on to the Bulli Pass and cut back to Scarborough. Of course there was always a chance that the road would be damaged in more than one place, and that the villages along that stretch — Coalcliff, Scarborough, Wombarra — would be isolated completely. I told myself it'd take more than a few hours of rain to do this but I wasn't convinced. The further south we went the heavier the rain got and we started to pass cars stalled alongside the road or sitting it out. Some hope.

At Engadine the road was awash and we had to plough through water axle-deep. The car in front of me didn't make it but I did. I waited for the fatal feel of water in the electrical system that'd bring this enterprise to an abrupt halt, but it didn't come.

'Good car,' Geoff said. 'Mine'd be stopped a couple of Ks back there.'

I grunted something in reply, but I was concentrating on just seeing and steering. The light was bad and the rain was like a gauzy curtain across the road. South of Engadine, the wind got up and the rain was driven against the car with a force that made you think you were out to sea in a twenty-knot gale with ten-metre waves. Even young, cool Geoff got alarmed.

'What's your visibility?' he asked.

'Poor to zero.'

'Shouldn't you stop?'

'Probably.'

He said nothing more and my admiration for the kid continued to climb. I turned on the radio again and found that the National Park route to the Illawarra was closed at the weir. I pushed on at a snail's pace to Stanwell Tops and was relieved that the rain and wind seemed to have eased slightly as we ran up to the junction that brings you down onto the coast road.

'Ever been here before, Geoff?'

'No.'

'Great view from the top here on a good day.'

But this wasn't anything like a good day; in fact it was more like the worst day. Instead of being able to see the indented coastline all the way down to Wollongong, all that was visible was sheeting-down rain and a surging, seething sea that thundered against the rocks as if it was determined to bring the whole escarpment down.

'Jesus,' Geoff said, 'that's wild.'

He had the right word. It was as if the forces that keep nature in check had suddenly let go and the pent-up energies of air and water were released in an assault upon the land.

'We'll never find anyone in this,' Geoff said as I began the winding descent to the coast. Cautiously.

'I told you. Look at it this way,' I said. 'If they're here, they're stuck here.'

'I guess. It was madness to put a road and a railway through here. It should've gone inland.'

'Tell that to the coal tycoons.'

He was right. The road clung to the very edge of the continent as if it had been stuck on with inferior glue. The sheer rock wall to the right in spots was crumbling and the signs that read FALLING ROCKS DO NOT STOP were a standing joke. 'Of course falling rocks do not stop,' people said. 'Unless they hit something.'

It was no joke now. The cyclone fence that protected the road to some degree from the falling rocks had been breached in several places and there was muddy debris across the rain-slick surface. Nothing sizeable so far, but it made every twist and turn in the road hazardous. The failing light and the increased velocity of the rain and wind didn't help.

'How far?' Geoff said and I could hear the fear in his voice.

'Not far. A few more turns. This is Coalcliff. The most vulnerable bit. Get past this and we should be right as far as the road's concerned.'

'What about houses and that?'

'It gets worse. Shut up and let me drive.'

We got around the last of the turns that had the rock wall threatening it and I could just see the 'Clifton' sign by the side of the road ahead. I heard Geoff breathe a sigh of relief and I didn't blame him. I hadn't said anything about it, but there hadn't been another car in sight during our descent and I strongly suspected that motorists had been warned to stay clear of the area.

The villages of Clifton and Scarborough seemed to be huddled down against the rain. The waves breaking on the rocks below the road were throwing up a spray that was blending with the driving rain. I crawled along until I found the road that crossed the railway line and led up to the flats below the escarpment. Mud was washing down the road and several large cracks had already appeared in it.

'Whole sections of this road are going to go,' Geoff said. 'The water undermines the road base which was probably pretty crappy stuff to start with. Jesus, look at that!'

I almost stopped and squinted through the downpour. People in yellow slickers were gathered around a fibro shack built on a steep slope. The shack was teetering. I crept past and over the drumming on the car roof heard the crack of timber and the sound of iron ripping away as the house left its moorings and slid towards the sea.

'Christ knows what it's going to be like in that slip area,' I said. 'If we can get there.'

A gust of wind tore several small trees from the ground and sent them spinning down a slope. Some larger trees were bent double against the gale and I felt the car rock several times before we turned a bend and were sheltered by a high rocky outcrop. The visibility was getting worse by the second as the light faded and the rain intensified. Suddenly the bitumen was gone. I skidded around a muddy bend, slid off the track and came to rest in a clump of sheoaks. The car stalled. I started the engine with some difficulty and gunned the motor. The wheels spun. Bogged.

My eyes had been adjusting to the murk and suddenly they didn't need to. A lightning flash momentarily lit everything as bright as day. I could see the slushy track to our left that was like a running gutter, the sodden bark on the dripping trees. The light glinted on a cyclone fence that told me we were near the old mine entrance and not far from where the slip had demolished the cottages years ago. Further ahead I could see a torrent pouring across the track. Another flash showed me the dashboard of the car, my hands locked to the steering wheel and Geoff's young, pale, stressed face. Then the thunder rolled in and there was no point in saying anything as the rain hammered on the roof.

When the thunder eased to a steady roar, I

leaned towards Geoff and shouted, 'I know where we are.'

'Great.'

'And we're staying here a while. Go out there and we're likely to be heading towards New Zealand.'

'Are we safe here?'

It was as if night had fallen, suddenly and early. I could hardly see a thing a few metres from the car, it was rocking but not sliding and the sheltering and anchoring presence of the sheoaks was a comfort.

I waited until a gust of wind had passed us by, shaking the trees but not moving the car. 'Nowhere's safe in this,' I shouted. 'But this's as good as anywhere.'

He rolled a cigarette and at that moment I knew I wouldn't object to the soothing smells of tobacco and marijuana in the car. Hell, I might even take a drag.

'Try the radio,' Geoff said.

I turned the ignition on and hit the radio button. Static, lots of static, then nothing at all. I tried the interior light. No.

Geoff lit the cigarette, cracked the window an inch, and then quickly closed it as the rain pelted in. 'I guess we're not driving anywhere even if we wanted to.'

I produced the whisky. 'I've got this and you've got your tobacco and grass.'

He rooted around in his backpack and came up with a large block of chocolate.

'Hey,' I said. 'Remember that guy who survived

in a snow cave in the Himalayas on a Mars Bar. We're better off than him.'

Geoff took a deep drag and exhaled. The sweet smell filled the car. 'Sure,' he said. 'Except that his mother wasn't dying of cancer, his sister wasn't running around with a murderer and he wasn't with a guy who didn't have a fucking clue what he was going to do next.'

24

We spent the night in the car. The rain hardly let up at all and we both got soaked when we ventured outside to piss. I shone the torch and confirmed that we were safer here than anywhere else. There was some protection on the west side; the ground underneath was firm and the trees were strongly rooted. All around us it seemed that this little sliver of Australia was sliding towards the sea. But we were okay.

We both slept in snatches, wet as we were. We shared the chocolate and the whisky, with Geoff having more of the one and me more of the other. It'd been a long while since I'd spent the night in a car and the last time I'd resolved never to do it again. Now I remembered why. I was stiff in every bone and the time dragged. When the first streaks of light appeared in the sky I felt like cheering although there was nothing to cheer about.

We shivered in those peculiarly cold first seconds after dawn, although we were both warmly dressed — me in my leather jacket and Geoff in his plus the parka. Geoff seemed to be dozing so I checked the .38, but he suddenly spoke.

'D'you think you'll need that?'

'I hope not. Does it bother you?'

'Yes.'

'Good. So it should, but I haven't shot anyone on my side for years.'

Not much of a joke, but the best I could do with locked joints, a stiff back and a ricked neck. I used the torch to study the map. I wasn't looking forward to slogging through the rain and mud looking for someone who mightn't even be there, but I did want to get out of the car. When I felt I could see well enough to keep my footing, I opened the door and stepped out into the wet world.

Geoff got out the other side and turned his back to the wind. The rain was still falling but not as heavily as it had during the night.

'Bugger it!' He slammed his mobile shut. 'Batteries.'

'Use mine.'

He took it from the glove box and I moved away while he made the call. Water from the trees dripped down my neck but I was so damp it hardly mattered.

The car door slammed. 'No change.'

'Let's get going. I think I've got my bearings. The shacks are down here. We can follow the fence and then work our way right.'

Following the fence meant, in fact, hanging onto it. The ground was so slippery and muddy that, even in my hiking boots, I slithered rather than walked. Younger, lighter and fitter, Geoff didn't have to grab at the fence so often, but he fell once and muddied himself all down one side. The fence turned left and we had to go right. There was an old track that had once had a layer of coal scree over it. Now it was a black, gooey mess we inched along beside rather than on. The water was ankle-deep in spots and where there was no tree shelter the wind whipped us in wet gusts.

I pointed. 'Down there.'

Three fibro shacks, or rather two and a half, clustered in a clearing in the middle of a steeply sloping sea of mud. Fifty, maybe sixty metres away. Geoff didn't seem to be paying attention so I pulled at his sleeve, but he was looking back up and to the south. He pointed.

'What?'

'By that big rock.'

I peered through the rain.

'Van,' Geoff said. 'Covered with a tarp.'

He was right and I felt my pulse rate go up a notch as I looked at the greenish, humped shape. I nodded and turned my attention back to the shacks. There obviously hadn't been any intention to re-build them after the initial damage; stumps had collapsed, sending them skewwhiff, and iron was missing from the roofs. On one, a deck had fallen away and hung off the structure like a rickety fire escape. The far one looked to be in the best condition with a more or less intact roof, several intact windows and a couple of long props holding a skillion in place. It had a deck that had once run around three sides. Only two sections remained and one was poised over a gully where

197

the water from higher up roared down at break-
neck pace. I could see sizeable rocks rolling in
the water along with tree branches and other
debris.

I took out my Swiss army knife and handed it
to Geoff.

He was too surprised not to take it. 'What the
fuck's this for?'

'You're going up to the van. I want you to
disable it anyway you can.'

'What're you going to do?'

'Flush him out.'

'I want to help.'

'You *will* be helping.'

'No way. I . . .'

'You'll do as I say, Geoff. That was the deal,
remember? We're almost there. Talbot'll be tired,
wet, cold and hungry most likely. And scared. I
won't have any trouble with him.'

'What about . . . her?'

'She'll be all right.' I shoved him hard. 'Get
going.'

He moved off up the slope towards the van.
When I was sure he'd committed himself, I began
to work my way down towards the shacks. There
was no substantial cover — just a few scruffy
bushes, an almost rusted-away car body and a dis-
integrating heap of timber and rubble that had
once been an outdoor dunny. I made all the use
I could of the cover and slowly, wetly — slithering
and bent double — reached the back of the shack
where a decayed set of wooden steps had been
reinforced by several brick-filled milk crates.

I took out the .38, tested the milk crates for stability, went up them and turned the door handle. It swung in with a loud creak but the rain had got heavier and the pounding on the iron roof would've drowned anything but a heavy metal band. For the first time I thanked the rain. The house was a ruin; cracks in the walls, gaps in the floor, sloping door jambs. It smelled of mice, rot and damp. I was in what had been a kitchen, but the equipment had been stripped out and the only piped water came from a hose from the outside running into a pipe where the sink had been. The roof leaked and there was plenty of water on the floor. I checked two uncloseable doors, one on either side of the passage after the kitchen. One room empty, the other full of rubbish.

I heard sounds coming from the front room and paused outside a door more or less fitted in its frame. A radio was playing and a man was raising his voice above the music and the noise of the rain.

'Turn that fuckin' thing off. I want to fuckin' talk to you.'

'I don't want to hear it. I don't want to hear any more of your bullshit.'

I shoved the door in and went into the room with the gun held down by my leg but in clear view. Megan French was lying on a mattress. A portable radio was by her side. She wore black — jeans, boots and a sweater. Talbot was standing over her, awkwardly angled with his back to me. He heard me come in, spun around and had to grab the wall for support.

'Who the fuck? Jesus, the fuckin' private eye.'

'That's right. This is the end of the run, Talbot. The police're on their way.'

He was tall and lean in mud-splattered white overalls with a denim jacket over them. He was unshaven and the dark stubble gave his narrow face a saturnine look. His eyes were shrewd as he backed up to the wall. 'Bullshit. You've come for her. Well, you can have her. Just leave me alone.'

'Damien.'

'Shut up! Fair trade? Her for me?'

'No trade, Talbot. Megan, your mother sent me to get you.'

She'd been lying down until that one word — mother — brought her upright. She sprang from the mattress. I could see the athleticism that had carried her over Tadpole Creek so easily, but her dark, beaky face was twisted with rage.

'Mother! Some fuckin' mother. That stuck-up bitch abandoned me at birth.'

'Yeah! Tell 'em, Meg.'

Talbot was high on something or perhaps coming down. His hands were clenching and unclenching as he flexed muscles in his arms and shoulders. He was going to be hard to control.

'You can talk to her about that,' I said. 'Just come with me, both of you.'

'No!' She threw herself in front of Talbot, who'd been waiting for something just like this. He grabbed her around the throat in an arm lock and took something from the bib pocket of his overalls. A click and a twenty-centimetre blade was against her throat.

'Put the gun down or I'll take her head off.'

I wondered if he had the strength to hold her. She looked physically capable of contesting with him, but the knife made the difference. He had the point under her chin and she could feel it.

'You're in trouble, Talbot,' I said. 'I mean over the guard. But it's not the end of the world. If you let Megan go and come with me it'll be better for you. Something in your favour. You're looking at prison but not forever. Harm her and it's entirely different. Kidnapping plus more violence and you'll be lucky to be out before you're fifty.'

'Fifty,' he sneered. 'Who cares about fifty.'

'You will, believe me.'

'Believe you? That's a joke. I haven't believed anyone but myself for . . .'

'You're talking to yourself. Stop it! Let her go. She hasn't hurt you.'

'The fuck she hasn't. Everyone's hurt me and I'm just starting to hurt back. If you want her still breathing drop the fuckin' gun!'

There was no chance I'd let him have the gun. I ejected the magazine and threw it back into the passage. I dropped the gun onto the mattress and came forward.

'Stay there!' he yelled.

I stopped. I had to keep him talking, shake him somehow and give Megan a chance to get away. 'What happened between you and the doctor, Talbot?'

'That fat bastard. He lied to me like everyone else. He promised me . . . Back off!'

'But he cut you loose when you killed the guard, right?'

He wasn't listening and Megan wasn't doing anything constructive. Talbot slid along the wall towards the French windows that gave out onto the deck. He was stronger than he looked, dragging Megan with him easily and keeping the knife where it belonged.

'Smart arse. Fuckin' smart arse. We're leaving and you're not going to stop us.'

Then I realised that she wasn't resisting. She was going along with him. They reached the windows and Talbot leaned his weight against them. They sprang apart and the wind billowed Talbot and Megan's clothes as they backed out onto the deck. I picked up the empty gun and followed. I had a spare magazine in my jacket but this didn't seem like the time to produce it.

The wind was howling and the whole building shook as gusts hit it. The deck was in as ruinous a state as the rest of the house and Talbot's boots slipped as he moved towards the corner of the house. There had to be some way down at the side — steps or a ladder — but I hadn't seen it. This wasn't too bad, Megan wasn't fighting him but where could they go? If this continued on up to the van the odds'd be even.

'There's nowhere to go, Talbot,' I shouted. 'Your van's been disabled.'

'I'll take your car or whatever I can find.' He cut her and the blood ran down her neck. I don't think she felt it. She was going with him, backing around the corner.

'Megan. Your brother's up there. He . . .'

She screamed: 'I haven't got a brother! I haven't got anybody!'

She pushed away from him like a middleweight breaking a lightweight's clinch, and came at me with her fingers spread, thrusting at my eyes. I side-stepped and she hit the wall with a force that made the deck shake. Talbot lunged forward, then grabbed the rail and moved back around the corner. I slipped and skidded after him. The full force of the wind hit him; he staggered and the rail gave way. He went over the edge into the roaring torrent and disappeared.

'Damien! No!'

Megan French came up beside me, shoved me aside like something weightless and for a moment I was sure she was going to jump from the deck into the surging water. I grabbed her arms and held her but there was no need. She sagged against me and I helped her back into the house. She dropped down onto the mattress and squatted there with her knees drawn up and her head in her hands.

'He can't swim,' she said.

I crouched, careful not to loom over her. 'It wouldn't matter,' I said. 'Not in that.'

'I nearly jumped in.'

'I know, but you didn't.'

I found myself minutely examining my feelings and reactions. I felt protective, relieved that she was safe, and slightly self-congratulatory that I'd seen things through to this point. Did I feel anything else? Paternal? I didn't know. I couldn't tell. Up close, wet and bedraggled as she was, the resemblance to Eve wasn't striking. Professional instincts were taking over — she was a young woman, the subject of my enquiries, and in trouble.

She rubbed the sleeves of her sweater across her eyes, face and hair and looked at me. 'What now? Police?'

'I don't know. What happened with the guard?'

'It was a sort of accident really. Damien challenged him and the guard hit him with his torch. Damien lost his cool and took the torch away and . . .'

'Did you see this?'

'No. That's what Damien told me. He was sort of pleased to have killed someone at last. Always knew he would. But he was scared, too.'

'Why did you go with him?'

She shrugged.

'Megan . . .'

'Get fucked. Who're you that I should tell you things?'

That's when I made a decision. 'Listen,' I said. 'You can come with me and see your mother and try to behave like a human being. If you do that I'll try to protect you. Or I can just throw you to the cops as Talbot's accomplice. Your choice.'

Too hard, I thought as soon as I'd said it. *She's too young to handle stuff like that.* But I was wrong. The real measure of a person is in terms of what he or she has been through and Megan French had been through a lot. She looked around the dilapidated room and the few possessions she and Talbot had brought into it. Blood was still trickling from the cut but she was unaware of it.

'I used to come here when I was a student.'

'I know. Your ... Mrs French, told me. That's how I got here. She cares about you.'

'Jesus, you really have been digging, haven't you? What's your name?'

'Hardy. Cliff Hardy.'

She sniffed and wiped her nose on her sleeve. 'Don't tell me she's pissed that bastard off?'

'Her husband? No, she just got away from him for a bit. Just long enough.'

'Poor dumb thing. If I go along with you, what about Damien?'

'He'll be found and it'll be over.'

'What about me?'

'Things can be arranged. But I have to know a bit more. What did Dr Macleod promise Talbot?'

She looked at the duffel bag on the bed that had apparently belonged to Talbot. There was a packet of tobacco, a lighter, a paperback book. It wasn't much to leave behind.

'He said he'd set up a sort of conservation foundation with Damien as its head. He really did care about conservation, but ... but he cared about smack more. The doctor supplied him.'

'Okay. What's it going to be?'

'This is just a job for you, right?'

I could see and feel her gathering strength,

sorting things out, making decisions and I wanted to help her, confirm the strength she was mustering, but I held off.

'That's right. A job.'

'I hope you know what you're doing then.'

25

I recovered the magazine for the .38 and made sure I'd left no signs of my presence in the house. Megan gathered up her things and didn't touch anything of Talbot's. She didn't speak or look at me. She behaved as if I wasn't there and that she was doing things of her own choosing in her own way. She was passive, remote. I was wary.

The rain had eased to a wind-whipped drizzle. Geoff was waiting by the van which was sitting up on its still-inflated tyres. He and Megan looked at each other as if each was a specimen in a glass jar.

'Megan,' I said. 'This is Geoff Samuels.'

Geoff handled it well. He nodded neutrally to her, took a clean handkerchief from his pocket and handed it to her. She pressed it against the cut. He gave her just enough attention before turning to me. 'Where's Talbot?'

I pointed to the roaring channel. 'He fell in. Drowned.'

Geoff took my knife from his jacket pocket and handed it to me. 'I didn't think it was a good idea to disable it. I thought we might need it.'

'Okay,' I said. 'But we don't.'

I had the flask with a last inch in it in my pocket. I moved closer to the van for shelter, took out the flask and drained it.

'I saw you and . . . your mother one day,' Megan said. 'What's wrong with her?'

'Cancer,' Geoff said. 'She's dying. She might be dead now. She wanted to meet you before she died.'

'Why?'

'Unfinished business,' I said. 'Come on, we'd better get going.'

We got the Falcon unbogged and started, more due to Geoff's skill than mine. I dug and pushed, he fiddled. The rain got heavier and all signs that we'd been there were rapidly washing away as we inched down the track or what was left of it. I let Geoff drive and he did it well, taking the bends slowly and keeping the revs up when we had to negotiate hub-high water. Megan sat quietly in the back with her bag and I had to stop myself from turning around to look at her. I wasn't sure why I wanted to look at her. Was I afraid she was going to jump out, or was I still asking myself that question? I did sneak one quick look. She was staring out the window. Her expression was blank and with her short hair and rain-washed face she looked young but not afraid.

Surprisingly, the coast road was still open and we drove to Thirroul where Geoff got batteries for his mobile and a mechanic complimented him on the job he'd done on the car and added a few touches of his own. It was still early and, as the rain eased, a few more vehicles appeared and people in slickers carrying umbrellas came onto the streets. Wet and muddy though we and the car were, it was nothing remarkable. I bought three coffees and cups of hot chips and we sat in the car and let the windows steam up.

'Tell me how it happened,' Geoff said.

I told him.

Megan said, 'He wouldn't have hurt me. He was scared. You heavied him. It's your fault he's dead.'

The rain had washed the blood from the cut on her neck and she'd tied the handkerchief over it, but blood was still slightly oozing. 'He cut you,' I said.

She fingered the wound and winced a little. She hadn't been aware of the pain until then. She said again, but with less conviction, 'He was scared.'

'We were all scared. It was a bad situation.'

She'd eaten her chips and drunk most of the coffee. She looked at the containers as if wondering where the contents had gone. Then she looked at me. 'Why were you scared? You had a gun.'

'I was afraid for you.'

'Why?'

I didn't answer. I finished the coffee and wished I hadn't finished the whisky. Geoff was outside, leaning on the car and smoking. I rapped on the window. He dropped the butt, stood on it, got back in and started the engine.

'Where're we going?' Megan said.

'To the hospital. To see your mother. Geoff, what're they saying at the hospital?'

I knew he'd phoned while I was getting the food and drink. 'Annie says to come straight away. She's pissed off at me for not being closer. She says it won't be long.'

We got on the road and a new set of questions began to nag at me. Should I have got the police in on it? Was I a bit drunk after most of a pint of whisky and not much to eat when I'd gone into the house? Could I have handled it better? Should I have shot Talbot in the leg straight away? What about his knife? What had happened to it? I wrestled with these things as Geoff drove, his face set like stone, back through the rain to Sydney.

We got to the hospital by early afternoon and went straight up to Cyn's room, Geoff and I drawing some looks for our muddy boots and clothes, tangled hair and unshaven faces. Anne was sitting close beside the bed holding her mother's hand. She looked up at us and her eyes widened when she saw Megan. But she was too involved in what was happening in the here and now to care about the past or the future.

Geoff whispered, 'I'm sorry, Annie. I . . .'

Anne, who looked a lot less glossy than when I'd first seen her, older and stronger, too, shook her head. 'It's all right, Geoffrey. You're here. She's almost gone. She can't really see or hear much.'

I heard Geoff draw in a deep breath and then he moved up behind his sister and rested his hand on her shoulder. Megan stood beside me. She was breathing heavily and her right hand was up, probing at the cloth around her neck. I wondered how she was going to cope with this after all she'd been through in the last few days. I wanted to offer her some comfort, physical support, but I knew better. She gripped the rail at the end of the bed.

Cyn's face was as white as the sheets and drawn in as if the bones had crumpled. Her eyes were closed and her mouth was just partly open. There was a slight rise and fall in the sheet over her body. Very slight. We stood there for what seemed like half an hour but was probably only a few minutes.

It was their moment and I felt I didn't belong. I was about to go out when Cyn's eyes opened wide. She looked at her daughter, at her son, and then made an effort to see more. Anne, best equipped now to know what was happening, beckoned Megan forward. She moved like an automaton but got close enough for Cyn to see her. I looked down at the face of the woman I'd once loved so much and then fought with and hurt and was glad that at least in the end I hadn't failed her. Her sunken eyes fixed on Megan and then her head moved towards me a fraction and her pale lips, thinned out to nothing, formed in the shadow of a smile.

Somehow, I found the ability to speak. 'This is Megan, Cyn.'

I don't know if she heard me or saw me or understood, because she turned her head slightly to the side again and looked at Geoff and Anne.

There was some movement of the two hands on the cover, but whether it came from Cyn or Anne I couldn't tell. I backed away but not so far I couldn't hear the soft hiss of her last breath.

26

I learned from Smith of Millennium Security that they found Damien Talbot's van the next day and his body a day later. It was a couple of hundred metres from where he'd gone into the water and was battered almost beyond recognition. Almost.

Unlikely as it seemed, Anne Samuels took Megan French under her wing. Accompanied by a lawyer, they went to the police and Megan told them basically what she'd told me — that she hadn't been present when the guard was killed and had gone with Talbot under duress. She showed them the wound in her neck and claimed it had been inflicted some time before it actually was and that she'd got away from Talbot after that. The police closed the books on Talbot, putting his death down to suicide or accident.

I learned this from Geoff. His computer duly turned up and he came to collect it. 'Annie drilled her in what to say,' Geoff said. 'And it worked. No charges or anything. She's a strange one, that Megan.'

'Has she said why she ran off the rails? Why she took up with Talbot and why she stayed with him?'

We were in my ratty back courtyard on a mild dry day with the leaves blowing around the bricks and catching in the sprouting weeds. I had a glass of wine and Geoff had a joint.

'It's weird,' he said. 'Annie's not married and the bloke who's the father of her baby isn't in the picture. Would you believe it? She's hired Megan as a sort of live-in nanny for when the baby comes. They get along fine apparently.'

'You didn't answer my question.'

'Annie says Megan has told her but she says I wouldn't understand.'

'I wonder if I would?'

Geoff puffed on his joint and didn't say anything and didn't look at me.

'Geoff,' I said. 'Spit it out. What?'

'Megan doesn't want to know you, Cliff. She doesn't like you. Doesn't trust you.'

'Does she know . . .?'

He nodded. 'She says it doesn't make any difference. Maybe Annie's right. Maybe we wouldn't understand. My guess is child abuse. That's the explanation for everything these days, isn't it?'

Maybe. I could believe almost anything of Rex French. But it looked as if I wasn't going to get the answers to those questions, not quickly at least. I had difficulty sorting out my feelings about this young woman who, I now had to accept, was my daughter. How do you know if you feel paternal when you don't know how paternal feels? Especially about someone you don't know who doesn't want to know you. All I could do was wait and stay in touch with the situation through Geoff.

I was glad that Megan had accepted her half-siblings and been accepted by them. Maybe satisfaction over that was a paternal feeling in a way. I telephoned Frank French and told him that his niece was in good hands. He said he'd get the message to his sister-in-law. It was something.

I went to Cyn's funeral. It was a big affair with lots of people there from Cyn's other life. People I didn't know. Megan stayed close to Anne and I kept my distance.

Smith orchestrated things perfectly. The police moved in on the Tadpole Creek protest and closed it down. Examination of the site revealed four bodies of elderly people, all women, buried in deep graves. All this was kept hush-hush until the remains had been identified from dental records. The common link between them was that they were former patients of Dr Bruce Macleod who was arrested and charged with their murder. Smith kept me out of it and claimed that his investigators had made the link between Macleod, the site and the financing of the protest. I understand Miss Cartwright is going to give evidence against Macleod who, apparently, had some black marks against his name back in Britain.

For a supposedly smart operator, Macleod made some fundamental but understandable mistakes. Analysis of the remains showed that he'd apparently been experimenting with drugs and surgery designed to reverse Alzheimer's disease. The old people were his laboratory rats and well selected because they didn't have any attentive, caring relatives and when the cops learned that these missing oldies were dementia cases their interest and energy dropped. So far, so good. Macleod knew that disposing of bodies in the big wide world is chancy. A controlled environment is the go; but his controlled environment slipped from his control before he could do anything about it. The protest he backed was a holding action. With the Olympic juggernaut held at bay and only the protesters to deal with, he reckoned to have a fair chance of correcting his mistake.

Work at the site went ahead quickly and smoothly and the few press articles that attempted to make sinister connections between the Games and the 'Tadpole Creek Graveyard' were quickly forgotten.

I tried to get in touch with Tess Hewitt but her phone didn't answer and when I drove out to Concord one sunny day with my explanations and a forty-dollar bottle of red wine at the ready, I found a For Sale sign and a neighbour who told me she'd packed up and gone to the north coast. A while later I got a postcard from her from Byron Bay with Mae West on it and the inevitable caption. I think I will go up and see her sometime.